THEIR SCANDALOUS BRIDE

A BRIDGEWATER BRIDES NOVEL

LACEY DAVIS

Welcome to Bridgewater, where one cowboy is never enough! *Their Scandalous Bride* is published as part of the Bridgewater Brides World, which includes books by numerous authors inspired by Vanessa Vale's *USA Today* bestselling series. This is a steamy standalone read. Enjoy!

*A*lastair Fraser and his best friend Keegan Black rode toward the O'Reilly ranch, eager to speak to the foreman about buying several horses.

The hills of Montana were golden as the aspens turned a toasted yellow color before winter arrived. Following fellow soldiers Ian and Whitmore to Montana, he'd fallen in love with the beauty of the mountains.

Now he and Keegan owned a nice piece of land where they raised cattle. Recently, a gang of cattle rustlers was stealing their herd, little by little. They needed to catch the rat-thieving bastards.

"Did you see Martin and Daniel's son? That cutie is trying to walk and we haven't even found us a wife yet."

"These things take time," Alastair said. Keegan longed for a family and Alastair was not in any hurry.

Families could be painful. It would take a lot of trust for him to commit to a woman. He'd long ago seen the dangers of giving your heart to someone. Money and greed could drive people to do terrible things including cheat on each other.

Their horses meandered down the trail to the ranch that bordered their own property.

"You've been telling me that for years. We haven't shared a woman in six months and my dick is perpetually hard. I'm past ready."

Alastair turned and gazed at his friend. "You want to marry just any woman? What if she doesn't believe in the Bridgewater way? What if she's not agreeable to being shared between us? What if she's a cheat, a liar, or even scandalous? Is that what you want?"

Keegan sighed. "No, but in order to find the right woman, you have to put some effort into courting. When was the last time we courted a woman? For that matter, when was the last time we fucked a woman?"

With a sigh, Alastair knew the man was right. They had been spending their time making their ranch profitable, building a house, and helping their friends and fellow soldiers in Bridgewater establish their ranches or places of business.

The community was thriving and Alastair had no regrets about coming to Montana. All he'd left in Scotland was scandal.

Maybe it was time to start searching for a woman. After all, he did want a family and maybe even a wife.

"As soon as we catch whoever is stealing our cattle, we'll come to town and start the search. But it's not going to be easy."

Just the thought made him nervous.

As they swayed in their saddles, they came closer to the O'Reilly ranch. The foreman had advertised that he had two unbroken foals and they were ready to add to their stable. The horses would be trained in time for spring roundup. Alastair and Keegan could also talk to him about his cattle situation. Was he losing cows or were they the only ones that were missing cattle?

The O'Reilly ranch butted up against their property, but the only person they had spoken to was the foreman. The original owners had died in a blizzard a few years back and now their daughter owned the land.

And from what he heard, she was a spitfire no one wanted to deal with. The rumors of her escapades were well known.

In school, she set the teacher's desk on fire. At church, the communion was exchanged for cake and the dressmaker refused to work with her after she cut the bodice out of the gowns.

The woman was a mischief maker with no one to control her. Though Alastair had never met her, she was not on his list of possible candidates for a wife. That kind of drama had no room in his life. None.

"Charley said to come to the barn," Keegan said as they rode through the gates of O'Reilly's Folly.

A large house sat not far from the barn. The ranch was a large piece of property and Alastair wondered about the woman who lived here. How could a woman handle this ranch?

They rode up to the barn and he swung a leg over his red mare. The horse had been his favorite for many years, but he knew in order to keep their stable secure, they needed to bring in new blood.

An older man with a limp came out of the barn, his gray hair covered by a large hat. "Hello."

"Alastair Fraser," he said, stepping up and gripping the man's hand.

"Keegan Black," his partner said doing the same. "We're here about the fillies you have for sale."

The man smiled. "Come on back here. Two of the sweetest little fillies. Their mother is out in the field if you want to take a look at her. And their papa is being ridden by Miss Catriona, though I expect her back soon."

It would be nice to see what their parents looked like, if they were in good shape.

They walked through the barn, the smell of leather and horses pervaded the area, though the doors were open on both ends of the structure.

They walked up to a pen where the two animals stood gazing about. The one neighed loudly.

"They're upset that I haven't moved them to the horse pen this morning. They like to run."

The two animals stood side by side. They were pretty little foals and he knew they would take a lot of work to train. Work they would do this winter.

"Let me take them out to the horse pasture and you can see them run," Charley said.

As he led them out, the man glanced at them. "Where you men from?"

"Bridgewater," Keegan said.

The man smiled and nodded his head. "Hear that's a real good place to live."

"We like it," Alastair said. "Your land butts up against ours."

For a second, the man paused walking and turned to look at them. "Really? I didn't know who owned that parcel. You know Phillip Johnson owns the land on the other side of us." The man sighed and continued walking toward an enclosed pasture. He pulled the rope from around the animals' necks and slapped them on the butts. They took off running.

As they watched the animals kick up their heels and gallop about the ring, Alastair knew they would be perfect for their stable. They would bring young blood into the group and would make excellent horses once they were broken.

For the next five minutes, they discussed money and when they reached an agreeable amount, he glanced at Keegan who gave him a nod.

"I'd like to see their mother and father," he said. "If they're healthy, then we have a deal."

The man smiled. "Well, the father is racing toward us right now."

Alastair glanced up to see a woman riding across the fields on a beautiful black stallion, her auburn hair flying out behind her. Riding astride, her skirts were raised to her knees, exposing long shapely limbs. His dick sprang to attention.

The scandalous Miss O'Reilly.

Like a punch to the gut, it was all he could do not to take a sharp intake of breath. Racing, the horse jumped the fence and came to a stop right in front of them.

The woman dropped to the ground and settled her skirts around her.

"Hello," she said breathless, and his imagination had her spread beneath them, her voice breathy as she came.

The woman was a stunning beauty, and though he knew she was wild, he couldn't help but think of fucking her.

"Hello," Keegan said as he stepped forward. "What a beautiful animal."

Oh no, he wasn't talking about the horse, Alastair

knew he was thinking about the woman. And he was right. The woman was gorgeous.

The way she rode that horse, no wonder they called her scandalous.

"Are you here about the foals?"

"Yes," Alastair said, wanting to restrain his friend, but knowing he could see the lust in the man's eyes.

"Great. They're such sweet girls. This is their father, Whiskey, and their mother Jasmine is the red mare in the yard."

Keegan didn't look at the horses but continued staring at the woman.

This couldn't be good.

"We'll take them," Keegan said.

The woman smiled. "Great. Now if you'll excuse me, gentlemen, I must get ready to attend the barn dance tonight. Are you attending?"

Oh no. Alastair wanted to grab his friend and run.

"We'd love to. Where is it being held?" Keegan said, turning and glancing at Alastair.

Her emerald eyes sparkled and the sweetest laughter rippled from her and it was all Alastair could do not to keep from seeing if her full lips tasted as sweet as they looked.

She was dangerous.

"In town at the city barn. I'll be looking forward to seeing you," she said as she turned and walked away.

Charley watched her stroll away. "That girl is like a

daughter to me. She needs a husband to protect her. There's a man in town who's already claimed her, so I would be careful if I were you."

The man was warning them away and that made Alastair curious.

Keegan glanced at Alastair. "No doubt, sir. A woman like that is bound to be snatched quickly."

After they paid the man, Charley promised to deliver the horses tomorrow, so they could attend the dance. Not that Alastair wanted to go, but he knew Keegan was eager to.

As they rode through the gates of O'Reilly's Folly. Alastair glanced at his partner.

"A dance was not in our plans for today."

"No, but you said we could start thinking about finding us a woman, and today it seemed like we'd been given the perfect opportunity. I'm going. What about you?"

There was no way he would allow Keegan to go and find a woman without him being there. The man seemed almost desperate and he needed to save his friend. Women were dangerous and deceitful.

"We'll go, but it's just a dance and we're not there to meet women," Alastair said.

"But Catriona, oh my goodness. My dick was jumping inside my pants."

Alastair laughed. "Your dick is always jumping at the sight of a pretty woman."

"All that red hair and those green eyes were gorgeous. The woman was spirited and I could just imagine her spread beneath us."

"She's trouble," Alastair said. "I'm not going to get involved with trouble. You know what happened and I won't accept a woman like that."

They continued riding when suddenly a man on a horse stepped in front of them.

Alastair pulled his mare to a halt.

"Hello, lads. How are you doing today?"

"What can we do for you?" Keegan said, his hand moving close to his pistol.

The man grinned in a way that sent a spiral of fear down Alastair's spine. Not that he was afraid of him, but the man was up to no good.

"What were you doing at the O'Reilly place?"

What? Why did he care what they were doing there? That was really none of his business.

"We bought a couple of fillies," Keegan said not in a friendly tone.

The man nodded. "Charley is still selling the damn horses. I'm going to have to make him stop. If it's the two little ones, you can have them, but don't expect to buy anything else from the O'Reillys."

"Why not," Alastair said his eyes narrowing. Did the man know something they didn't?

"Cat is expecting my child. She's off limits and O'Reilly's Folly will soon be mine."

Nothing had been said about the woman being engaged and she'd ridden that horse not like a woman expecting a child.

"We bought a horse, not a woman," Alastair said, knowing he really didn't want to get involved with the woman now. Not only did she have scandal attached to her name, but she was expecting another man's child.

The man smiled at them, though his eyes were dark with warning.

"And what is your name?" Keegan asked.

"Phillip Johnson. I own the ranch next to the O'Reilly's and I plan on making it all mine."

Could this be why Charley had warned them?

"Good day," Keegan told the man and they rode around him.

As much as Alastair didn't want to get involved with Catriona, he couldn't help but feel disappointed. Sure, he knew she had dishonor attached to her name, but what he had heard was nothing more than childish pranks. But to be expecting another man's child made her off limits.

2

———

Catriona O'Reilly tried to ignore the gossips who had no idea what they were talking about. Sure she had done some outrageous things in her past, but nothing that would cause them to ignore her and not speak with her.

What was going on?

She glared across the barn dance floor at the man who she feared and determined he would never obtain her hand in marriage. She'd rather die than marry Phillip.

Normally, she was the most sought-after single woman at the dance, but not tonight. Tonight she stood along the barn wall watching the dancers, wishing she was one of them.

The older ladies were gathered in the corner

glancing at her and whispering. What were they talking about?

She felt a hand at her waist and she whirled around, her hand was raised to smack whoever was brave enough to touch her so intimately.

Phillip.

The man took her hand and grinned. "Dance with me."

"No," she hissed.

"Now, Cat, I've tried every way I can to get you to court me and you've refused," he said, pulling her out on the dance floor.

As much as she detested this man, she didn't want to cause a scene, so she let him take out onto the floor.

"I'll never marry you," she said.

It was then she noticed that everyone in the barn was gazing at them. Staring to see what would happen next and that was exactly what the man wanted.

The man laughed and smiled down at her. "Then you'll be an old maid. Because even now Stella is telling everyone that you're expecting my child."

She came to a halt in the middle of the dance floor.

"You're a liar," she said loud enough to be heard.

"Don't make a scene," he said, his eyes flashing with anger as he pulled her into his embrace.

"You'll never get away with this," she said. "I'm not marrying you. I don't even like you."

A smile creased his cheeks and his dark eyes glared

down at her. "I already am. Even now the old ladies are gossiping about you and the single men's mothers have warned their sons to stay away from a hussy like you."

It was true. The single men had avoided her all evening. And though she had not found any of them particularly enticing, she also knew that Phillip had damaged her reputation and would keep her from making a catch.

The only reason she wanted to marry was children and a family. After witnessing her parent's marriage, she wanted nothing to do with most men. Especially anyone who raised a glass of whiskey.

"So when should we make an announcement regarding our marriage," he said, grinning at her like he'd won.

The music came to an end and she leaned in close. "When hell freezes over."

She pulled away from him and marched over to the wall, seething. Then she glanced at the women, they were all whispering. Angrily, she strode over to them.

"Hello, ladies, I just wanted to warn you that you've been fed a line of bullshit."

They gasped.

"I know you're smarter than to believe that I would ever go to bed with Phillip. There's no bun in the oven. And in fact, I'm still as virginal as a newborn babe. So stop spreading Phillip's lies. We will never marry."

She turned and walked away, trying to fight back the tears that threatened to overwhelm her.

Just then the door opened and in walked the two men she'd met this morning. Tall with dark hair and blue eyes, Alastair was handsome, but distant. He'd watched her carefully all morning while Keegan's dark hair and beautiful dark brown eyes enticed her. He made her smile and she had the most irresistible urge to reach out and touch that firm chest of his.

There was an instant attraction to the men and she didn't know which one she would choose, but either one of them was quite enticing.

This morning, she'd enjoyed their flirtatious good looks and beautiful sparkling eyes and lips that were full, ripe, and ready to be kissed. Maybe they were the answer to her prayers.

Strolling across the dance floor, she weaved in and out of the dancers. "Hello, gentlemen. Would you care to dance?"

Yes, she was being bold and brazen, and frankly, she didn't give a damn. It was time to show Phillip that he would never win her hand in marriage, regardless of whatever bullshit lies he told about her.

A little shiver trickled down her spine as the rugged and handsome, Keegan took her hand. "Yes, ma'am. Let's dance."

"I wasn't certain you would be here tonight," she said, glancing up into his earth brown eyes. His long dark lashes were gorgeous and she could feel the strength of his embrace. Her breath seemed to hitch in her lungs and she had the urge to reach up and touch his full lips but resisted.

"Nothing could have stopped us from attending this dance. Not even some cowboy who claimed you were his fiancée," he said.

What? When had Phillip spoken to them.

"What?"

"Some man stopped us on our way out of your place and told us you were promised to him. Not to buy anymore horses from you."

That cad. He'd been watching her ranch? Could he be the one who was stealing her cattle?

"He's lying," she said. "He's spreading rumors about me and none of them are true. We'll never marry," she said. "What about you? Why hasn't some cowgirl claimed you? A big strong handsome man like yourself."

"Thank you, but I've been too busy working my ranch and have no time for women. But I think that's about to change."

She grinned. Maybe her luck was headed for the better.

"Only thing is I'm a Bridgewater man," he said low into her ear.

Bridgewater, that mysterious town not far from Helena where every woman had two husbands. She'd often wondered about that place and the people who lived there. When she saw the women in town with their families, their husbands were attentive, and she could see the love between them.

Was it wrong to want that kind of relationship with your husband? Even if you had more than one? All she wanted was a man to cherish her and love her and give her a family. But two husbands?

That was different. She thought of her own family and it couldn't be any worse than what she'd witnessed between her parents.

The song ended and Keegan escorted her over to his friend. "Alastair, she's a dream on the dance floor. Take a whirl."

She could see that the man was reluctant, but she wanted to experience each man. For some reason, she felt drawn to both. Grabbing his hand, she pulled him out on the makeshift wooden floor.

"Why don't you like me?"

"Who said I didn't like you?" he asked her.

"Don't you think I can tell?"

A smile spread across his face. "It's not that I don't like you, but I'm cautious when it comes to women. Especially women with a reputation."

She gave a little laugh. "Honey, if you think I have a reputation, you're sadly right, I do. Because I don't put up with any lying bullshit. And that man across the way over there thinks he can con me into becoming his wife. Now if you want to believe all the gossip, I suggest you go join those old biddies in the corner. I've become the center of their world since Phillip started spreading lies."

God, how she was beginning to hate Phillip. And yet, Charley seemed to be pushing her toward him. That had to end tonight.

"He met us right outside your ranch and told us you were engaged and expecting his baby."

It was almost funny, except it wasn't.

"Sweetheart, a man can lie about being a virgin, but a woman can't. And frankly, none of you men will ever learn the truth about me until there's a ring on my finger."

The expression on his face was almost comical as she watched him try to determine if she was lying or telling him the truth. The man didn't seem to want to trust her and that made her a little uneasy. Maybe this wasn't the solution to her problems. But he was so handsome that when he glanced at her, she just wanted to remove her clothes. A heat seemed to be building inside her.

Suddenly, Phillip, jerked her away from Alastair. "Didn't I tell you that she was my woman? That we were engaged? Why are you dancing with her?"

"Because I asked him," she said, noticing that everyone was staring at them.

Phillip grabbed her by the arm. "Get off the dance floor, now. While I take care of business."

"No, we're not engaged and never will be," she told him.

Alastair took a step back and shook his head. "I don't know what's going on between you two, but I want no part of it."

Whirling around, he walked toward the barn door.

"Alastair," she cried as she tried to run after him, but Phillip grabbed her arm.

"You're not going anywhere."

With a sigh, she watched Alastair grab his hat and coat and with Keegan, the two of them walked out the door.

There went her only chance at trying to find herself a husband. Someone that wasn't afraid of Phillip. Every other man in town believed the liar and had stayed clear of her.

Phillip laughed and tried to pull her into his embrace.

"Don't touch me," she said, jerking from his hold, and walked away.

The rest of the night, she leaned against the wall, but no other man had the courage to ask her to dance. Phillip had frightened them all away.

Finally, she gathered her things, disappointed. When she stepped outside into the dim light from the barn, a hand reached out and grab her. Another hand came across her mouth as she tried to scream.

"We're going to talk and you're going to agree to marry me," Phillip whispered in her ear. "I'm not going to put up with you flirting with other men. Do you understand?"

He pinched her arm hard and slapped her bare shoulders.

"Stop," she cried, realizing he intended to beat her into submission. But she wasn't going down without a fight.

One thing her worthless father had taught her was how to protect herself and she took his thumb and pulled back on it until it snapped. With a scream, he let go of her and she shoved him with all her might.

Phillip stumbled back and fell, his head smashing against a large rock. In the light, she could see blood spurting from his skull as he lay there unconscious.

Oh my God, she'd killed the man. She'd killed Phillip and no one would ever believe it was an accident.

Terrified, she fled to her wagon. She had to get home. Charley would help her. Charley would protect her.

3

That night when Catriona arrived home, Charley was sound asleep and she didn't have the heart to wake him.

All night long, she tossed and turned and worried she would soon find herself in jail for Phillip's murder.

The next morning, when she dragged herself out to the barn, Charley was getting ready to take the foals to Bridgewater.

"Did you have a good time last night?"

"No," she said. "Phillip told everyone I was expecting his baby and that we would soon marry. I don't like liars."

Charley frowned and stared at her. "The boy is smitten with you. While that's not a way to win a woman's affection, you should at least give him a chance."

Stunned, she stared at the man. Did he not see what she saw? Phillip was a bully. Since his father's death, his own ranch had gone downhill and there was an evilness about him that frightened her.

She knew he wanted O'Reilly's Folly, but she wasn't going to marry him. But why was Charley in favor of this man?

"It's hard to give a man a chance when he embarrasses you and then he tried to manhandle me when I went to leave."

She'd planned on telling Charley she might've killed Phillip, but something held her back.

Maybe it had been a bad dream and hadn't really happened. No, she'd seen the blood spurting from his head where he hit a rock when she pushed him. But maybe he wasn't dead. She hadn't checked his pulse.

Should she turn herself in?

"That's not right," Charley said. "Women don't like to be forced or manhandled in any way."

"No," she said, biting her lip.

The man frowned. "I was about to take these foals over to Bridgewater. But something has come up. I'm going to be busy today."

It was the excuse she needed.

"Let me take them for you," she said. "I'll make it back before dark."

A frown drew his forehead together. "You sure?"

"Yes," she said, fearing he would back out.

If she had killed Phillip, the sheriff would be arriving anytime now. This way, she could get away and maybe put off going to jail just a little longer.

Maybe Keegan and Alastair would help her. Maybe they would save her. Maybe they could take her somewhere where the law would not hang her.

"All right," he said. "Just be careful."

A smile crossed her face and she ran into the house to pack just a few things. Maybe they would let her stay.

4

*E*arly the next morning, Alastair covered their campfire as Keegan saddled up their horses. Neither man said a word, disappointment heavy in the air.

"I thought she was the one," Keegan said. Even if she had been pregnant, he would have married her. He would protect her and the baby with his dying breath. If he could, he would save every orphan in the world, but knew that was impossible.

"No, I told you there was too much scandal involved with that woman. Look at the scene we were a part of because of her. Maybe she's pregnant, maybe she's not, but I don't want to get involved with Catriona."

A sigh filled Keegan as he climbed up on his horse.

"Shouldn't take us too long to get home now. An empty house with no one to greet us at the door."

Alastair shook his head. "How do you know of these things? You were raised in an orphanage. Did you have people who greeted you at the door?"

Laughter came from Keegan at the absurdity of his comment. "Oh yeah, with cookies in hand," he said. "The only time we were greeted at the door was when something was wrong. Then we were gathered together until someone confessed that they had been bad. And we were all punished."

The days had been harsh and the nights long and Keegan would never let any child of his suffer that way. If he were killed, he knew Alastair would make certain his wife and children were cared for. It was one reason he liked the Bridgewater way.

The odds of both of them being killed at the same time was almost zero.

"One of the reasons I ran away at twelve was because I was tired of being beaten once a week. I didn't have much when I left, but I knew my life would be better from that day forward. And it has been. Especially after I joined the Mohamir army and met all my friends. You men have made me into a great person who now wants a wife and family of my own."

They rode along the established path to Bridgewater, each man swaying in his saddle, each deep in thought.

"Damn, she was so pretty and I loved her spirit," Keegan said out loud not really talking to Alastair, but knowing he'd never wanted a woman so badly.

When they danced, her body had fit perfectly with his and her curves had been a pleasure to watch. The woman had everything he wanted, including a smart, sassy full mouth that would be perfect for kissing.

"You're right. She had a strong, willful spirit that would have been a pleasure to tame in bed, but she's nothing but trouble. And I'm not going to be associated with any woman who has scandal on her hands. Even if Phillip was lying, that will follow her the rest of her days. I've had enough of that in my life."

Keegan knew his friend had suffered much when his family was driven from the village where they lived in Scotland.

"We'll search for another woman," Alastair said. "One that will not bring shame on our children. One that will not harm us in such a way that we want to run to escape the reality of what she's done."

Keegan bristled. "I'm not running from anything. Those days are behind me and if scandal were to be brought on us, I'm staying and fighting. Even if the truth were to hurt us, I'd rather face it head on."

Alastair didn't reply and Keegan knew he was thinking of his father. The man had a troubled past. Keegan was an orphan and Alastair's family was riddled with disgrace.

"I know you want a woman with a good reputation, but I would have married Catriona without a moment's hesitation. Even if she were pregnant with another man's child. All children need love and I plan on being the best father possible to any child that needs love."

There was a boy he took food to every time he went into town. If he ever settled down, he would love to bring him to their home and let him work for them.

Alastair nodded. "Your roots are showing."

"And so are yours," Keegan admonished. Both of them had been hurt and even damaged in some way by their parents. His, for leaving him on a street corner at the age of three. Alastair's for letting his mother destroy their lives.

Apparently, Alastair had enough of that topic when he asked, "Why did you let me forget to ask Charley about the rustlers?"

"Because we were both blinded by the beauty of Catriona," he said. "Once she rode into the yard, it was like my brain turned to mush and my dick took over. Nothing mattered but her."

"I can't deny she took my breath away."

They pulled up to their fence line and Keegan frowned. The herd count was down again. Once the new foals arrived, they would gather the men of Bridgewater and catch this thief and find out why he was stealing from them.

"More are missing," he said out loud.

"Yes, that sweet little heifer with the star on her chest is gone," Alastair said. "Damn, that makes me mad."

"Me too. We work hard and don't deserve to be stolen from."

It had taken Keegan years before he'd felt like he had put poverty behind him and he had no plans on ever returning to living on the streets ever again.

Turning their horses, they rode into the bustling town of Bridgewater. A sense of homecoming came over Keegan and he knew he would live here until his dying day. It felt good to be home. Back to the place where they loved the people who lived here.

"When Charley brings our new horses, you can ask him about the rustlers then," Keegan said.

"Good idea. He should be here later today," Alastair said.

"Let's put our horses in the barn, rub them down and give them a bag of oats. Then we can see if one of the wives has room for two more at her table," Keegan said. "I'm ready for some good food and I know our women always prepare a delicious meal."

Alastair turned and stared at him. "If it's not sex you're thinking about, it's food."

"Aye, you're right. I'm hungry all the time and if I can't have the beautiful woman I want, then give me a good meal to satisfy my urgings."

"We may need to go to the whorehouse in Helena if

you keep on this way," Alastair said as they rode their horses into the barn.

Thirty minutes later, they carried their saddle bags with them as they walked out into afternoon sun.

"Let's go find something to eat," Keegan replied.

Suddenly Alastair stopped and shielded his eyes from the sun. "My oh my, look who is coming to visit."

Keegan jerked his head in the direction they had just come. "Catriona."

"She's bringing our new foals," Alastair said, shaking his head. "Here comes trouble."

5

___

*A*lastair walked up to her horse and helped her alight. "What are you doing here, woman?"

She licked her lips nervously as she stared at the man before her. The way he called her *woman* sent a trickle of some unknown desire skittering down her spine to her center. And she knew he didn't even really like her.

"I brought you your foals," she said, not wanting to spill her problems to them just yet. What if they didn't want her? What if they sent her back to Helena? What if they turned her over to the law?

"Why didn't Charley bring them?"

She didn't want to tell them the truth.

"He was busy and asked me to."

And she hoped and prayed that her home would still be standing when she returned. There were horror stories of how entire towns came after someone for a killing and destroyed their homes. It was all she had left and while her memories were not pleasant there, it was still a roof over her head.

"It's getting late," Keegan said as he walked up to her. "You can't return to your ranch tonight."

She closed her eyes. She didn't want to return to her home. She wanted to stay with these men. She wanted to remain here in Bridgewater and accept this lifestyle, but how did she know if they wanted her?

Alastair had not welcomed her and stood off to the side glaring at her like she had done something wrong, which she had. The man stared at her like he wanted to undress her one moment and like he hated her the next.

What had she done to cause his dislike?

"Can we talk somewhere private?"

The people in the small town were glancing at her with curious stares and she didn't want to spill her problems right here in the street.

Keegan took the foals and put them in the barn and then he tied her horse to a hitching post outside.

Alastair stood on one side of her and Keegan on another as they walked her to a house in the distance.

"Is this your home?"

"Yes, our ranch butts up against your property, but our house is here on the edge of town," Alastair said.

"Oh," she replied for the first time feeling nervous.

Would they help her? They must own a lot of land if their ranch butted up against hers.

When they walked inside, Alastair removed her coat and a gasp escaped from him. "What the hell happened?"

Keegan turned from the kitchen and glared at her. He walked over and lit a lantern and held it up to her arms and chest.

"Who did this to you?"

"The father of your child?" Alastair asked.

"No," she said. "I'm not pregnant. Phillip did this to me last night. That's why I'm here. I'm in trouble."

Keegan gave a small chuckle.

"I knew it," Alastair said. "I told you she was pregnant."

She whirled around and faced Alastair. "Listen, I'm not pregnant. Don't believe his lies."

"Let the girl talk," Keegan said.

For the next five minutes, she preceded to tell them what happened after they left. How Phillip attacked her when she walked out the door and she fought him off. How she broke his thumb and then pushed him away. Only instead of falling to the ground, he'd landed on a rock and now she feared she had killed him.

Alastair groaned and shook his head.

Keegan sighed. "You are definitely in trouble. Did you go to the sheriff?"

"No, I haven't told anyone. Not even Charley. I'm hoping you will help me," she said.

The two men glanced at one another.

"Honey, tomorrow morning we're taking you to the sheriff," Alastair said, running his hand through his hair. "If Phillip is dead, you could soon be hanging."

Did the man want to see her hang? What had she done to him to make him dislike her?

"Why? He attacked me. He spread rumors about us and he insisted that I marry him. I'm never marrying that bastard." With a sigh, she sank down onto the couch and put her head in her hands. "All I want is to find a man to love me and raise a family, and instead I have this crazy man chasing after me. All he wants is my land. Not me."

They glanced at each other and then she began to cry.

"I didn't mean to hurt him, honestly."

They pulled her up from the couch and guided her between their bodies. Keegan held her while she cried. Alastair leaned against her back and she was sandwiched between them.

She'd never felt more protected than she did at this moment. Two men holding her, supporting her, and giving her comfort when she felt like her life was coming apart at the seams.

"You can spend the night here," Alastair said. "But in the morning, we'll all go to town and try to get this cleared up. In the meantime, do you know how to cook?"

She glanced at Keegan who grinned at her. "Sorry, we're bachelors and our own cooking is not great. We usually eat with one of the married couples. But tonight, we'd like to have you all to ourselves."

She licked her lips, her nerves suddenly overwhelming her. What did they mean have her all to themselves?

"Look, you two are really sweet, but we're not married and I'm not going to have sex with you. If that's what you want, I'm leaving right now."

Keegan glanced over her shoulder at Alastair and she could see that though nothing was said, they were communicating with one another.

"No, we're not going to have sex with you. What we mean by having you all to ourselves is that we want to talk and get to know you. You're not what we thought when we first met you."

"Oh, so you believed all the lies being spread about me," she said.

"You do have quite the reputation," Alastair said. "I know all about your deeds in the past."

The man caused her anger to rise as he stared at her so certain of her faults.

"Well, good for you. Is your past a shining example of pureness? I'm no different than any other woman. I'm not a loose woman and I don't like men who are dishonest. Have you ever been dishonest with someone?"

Alastair's eyes narrowed as he stared at her. "That's none of your business."

"I won't assume the worst about you if you don't about me."

She was sick and tired of being thought of as an unscrupulous woman and right now she'd fight any man who thought badly of her. Maybe it was time for men to have to lead a life of perfection. Would any of them pass the test?

Keegan chuckled. "Let's just eat some supper and see how tonight goes."

Why couldn't she find a man who wanted to court her and love her? Why did that seem so impossible?

Even with these men, she wondered if they truly believed in her innocence.

6

___

$\mathcal{E}$arly the next morning before the sun had risen, Alastair and Keegan left the house to go to the barn. It was time to feed the animals and get started on their day. Catriona was in the house fixing them breakfast and it all felt so surreal.

Alastair felt like at any moment a scandal would ensue and they would be forced to leave town.

"Kind of nice having a woman feed us," Keegan said.

"Yes," Alastair admitted, though he had barely slept all night long. Any moment, he thought he would hear the stairs creak and she would crawl into bed with them. Part of him wanted her to be that brazen and part of him resisted.

"Too bad she's not sharing our bed."

"We're taking her to town this morning and then

we'll return her to Charley. She has no business staying with us," Alastair admonished.

Though his dick thought differently, he sounded like an old man. Why couldn't he just take her and enjoy the pleasure he would find between her legs? Why couldn't he be like other men and just use women for sex?

Keegan grinned as the frozen grass crunched beneath their boots. "Are you telling me you're not attracted to her?"

That was the irony of the situation. Alastair wanted to fuck her so badly and yet she was the exact opposite of the type of woman he wanted. No matter what she said, he still did not believe she was innocent. He still believed she was pregnant and just trying to hoodwink them into marrying her.

With so much indignity attached to her name, they had something in common and he had tried for years to rid himself of the disgrace. Over half a continent away, he still had to keep his name clear of more rumormongering.

"I'd love nothing better than to raise her skirts, lay her over our table, and fuck her into next week. But I'm not going to give her what she wants. Last night, she admitted to us that she wants to get married and have children."

Shaking his head, Keegan stared at him, hopeful.

"All women want to get married and have children," Alastair said. "But most women don't have a bad reputation attached to their name. And I don't want a woman who I have doubts about her innocence. I wonder if she's fooling us. Am I wrong to want to marry someone I can trust?"

"No," Keegan said. "But if we were in Scotland and you were trying to find a bride, would there not be scandal associated with your name?"

Alastair tensed. The damn man was right. And yet it was the very reason he didn't want to marry Catriona. Though he felt drawn to her and even wanted to help her, he wasn't certain he could ever trust her.

"Yes, you're right. After our family's good name was mired in mud, I never want to experience that again. Catriona's name is tarnished and we don't know if what she's telling us is the truth or not."

He opened the door to the barn and the new foals stared at them as they each went about the tasks they performed each morning.

Keegan was silent for a moment. "Let's think about this logically. Phillip warned us to stay away from her because she was pregnant with his child and they were engaged to be married. Cat was riding a horse at full speed when we met her. If a woman was pregnant, wouldn't she be more careful riding?"

There was no denying what Keegan said was true.

"But there are other rumors about her," he said. "The one I find especially disturbing is the one she was caught swimming without her clothes and two men joined her in the swimming hole."

Keegan was silent. "That one I can't reconcile. I don't have enough information. But would you force a woman to marry you after she's made it known that she despises you?"

Alastair turned on his friend. "Never. So why is Phillip so determined that Catriona will be his wife."

"He either has a twisted mind or he wants her ranch."

There was that and with Catriona's parents both dead, she was an easy target. Oh how Alastair wanted to believe her, but then the past would remind him of everything he lost.

"I know her parents died in a blizzard. We need to ask her how they lost their lives," Keegan said.

The memory of Alastair's parents came to mind and he quickly shoved the unhappy thoughts away. They were the reason for his being so cautious about being married. He'd witnessed a disastrous union between two people who hated each other. And he wanted no part of such a marriage.

A marriage that tore his family apart.

"Why do you need to know how they died?" Alastair asked, thinking he didn't want to share with anyone the death of his parents.

The sun was peeking over the horizon, the rays shining across the land through the open doors of the barn. The start of a new day and yet he was still stuck in the past. Even though he'd moved to America, he'd brought his pain with him all the way from Scotland.

"Because it's obvious that Phillip wants to join their ranches together. Would he or could he have done something to harm her parents? Then she would be easy prey for him."

Alastair stopped filling the bucket with water, his mind churning away at the possibility of Phillip being implicated in their deaths.

"All right, we'll ask about how her parents died. But we're in agreement that we're taking her to Helena today. And that we're going to the sheriff?"

For Alastair's peace of mind, they had to take her in or find themselves embroiled in a murder if Phillip was dead.

Keegan was silent for a moment as he walked about inside the barn and went over to the new foals that gazed at him their big eyes filled with curiosity. He rubbed their heads and pulled out a carrot which he broke in two and gave each one.

"We've been friends, brothers, for so many years and we always agreed that we would find a woman and share her between us. I'd marry Catriona in a minute, but you're the more cautious one, so I'll defer to your opinion. But if we learn she's in danger, I'm going to marry her. I'm going to protect her."

Nothing had ever come between them before now.

And while Alastair understood and even agreed that he wanted to spread Catriona's thighs and have his way with her, he had doubts. Or maybe after his mother's scandal he could not trust any woman.

The thought caused his chest to ache and he pushed the troublesome images away. No matter what, he would not let his past ruin his future and yet he feared marrying Catriona would be like being wed to his past. Nothing but gossip.

"This is not something I would agree to, but because you're more my brother than my any of my blood relatives, I will consent to this. But only if she is in danger. And if we learn of more indignations before you wed her, I'll reject the idea of this marriage."

Keegan smiled at him. "Thank you. Guess we better get the animals fed and head to town."

A blood curdling scream echoed through the barn and the men hurried outside. Mattie Craghead stood in the middle of the street looking everywhere. "My son is missing. He's not in the house and I can't find him anywhere. Alex and Jessie are gone and..."

The woman broke down and started sobbing.

Keegan rushed to her side as other men came out of their homes. "We'll get a search team and start looking for him."

When it came to children, Alastair knew that Keegan had a heart as big as Montana. They were not going anywhere until this child was found.

7

———

Catriona heard the screaming. She had cooked eggs and bacon and even made homemade biscuits. Breakfast was all laid out. She ran out the door and saw Keegan comforting a crying woman.

She stood next to another woman and they stared at the scene.

"What happened?"

"Little two-year-old James is missing," she said, wiping a tear from her eye before she turned and glanced at Catriona. "I'm Georgia Hamilton, married to Daniel and Martin."

Though Catriona knew the reputation of Bridgewater, she had never met any of the women in person.

"Catriona O'Reilly," she said. "I'm just visiting."

The woman smiled at her.

For a moment, Catriona watched as Keegan

comforted the missing child's mother and then began to organize a search team.

"What's it like being married to two men?"

The woman glanced at her. "Are you considering Keegan and Alastair?"

With a sigh, she didn't know how to respond. "I'm very attracted to them, but I don't think they want me."

Georgia chuckled and rubbed her hand over her large pregnant belly. "I think you're wrong about them wanting you. Even now, I can see them looking over to make certain you're all right. All I can tell you is that my two husbands are my life. They look after me, they take care of me and do everything possible to make me happy. If you speak to any of the women here in Bridgewater, you'll learn we love our life here and would be so happy to see you marry Keegan and Alastair. Both are really good men. And Keegan, bless him, he loves children so much."

Catriona's chest tightened. It seemed like Georgia had exactly what she wanted. A loving relationship, but instead of one man, it was with two. As long as they were happy, she would be thrilled to have both Keegan and Alastair. But unfortunately, Alastair believed the worst about her.

This town, this world, was completely opposite from what she'd experienced as a child growing up. And yet it appeared a city of love. Families were now gathering outside, the women comforted the child's mother, the men prepared to go in search of the missing boy.

"They're getting ready to ride. I should give them the breakfast I made for them," Catriona said.

"If there is ever a time you want to talk, we live a few houses down. Come over and visit. I'd love to learn more about you and your men."

"Thank you, but they're taking me back to Helena today," she said. "But thank you for talking to me."

"Anytime," the woman said as she walked across the street to join the other women.

Catriona went into the kitchen and hurried out with biscuits wrapped in a napkin. She went to Alastair first.

"Maybe you can eat breakfast while you search for the boy," she said.

A stunned expression crossed his face. "Thank you."

She wanted to say so much more but didn't think this was the time to speak of things that troubled them.

"Find the child," she said.

"We will," he promised and turned his horse away.

Quickly she stepped over to Keegan and handed him his egg biscuit. "I brought you your breakfast."

Keegan sighed and shook his head. "He's so small. He must have tried to follow his father when he left this morning."

His eyes were teary and she could see how

concerned he was for the child. He genuinely cared and her chest tightened with pain for both Keegan and the missing child.

"You'll find him. I'm confident in your ability and your determination."

A weak smile crossed his face. "Thank you. I just hope we find him before he gets into real trouble."

The men were beginning to ride out. "Go. I'll say a prayer for the boy and for the men searching."

He took the biscuits and put them in his pocket. "Stay in the house."

"Of course," she said, knowing that she had planned on wandering around the small village and even speaking to some of the women.

Groups of men rode in different directions and she stood watching them leave.

A woman walked over to her. "Hello, I'm Emma. I'm married to Whitmore and Ian. And who are you?"

"Hello, I'm Catriona O'Reilly. I'm visiting Keegan and Alastair."

The woman smiled at her. "Keegan adores little James. He adores all the children. Of course, with his background I'm sure children have a special place in his heart."

"His background?" Catriona asked.

The woman ignored her comment. "How long are you going to be here?"

"They were taking me back to Helena this morning."

"Are you their girlfriend?"

If only, Catriona thought. She glanced about the streets of Bridgewater and noticed a small group of men had stayed behind.

"What is life like living here in Bridgewater?"

Emma took her hand. "Come to the house and we'll talk."

"Oh, I can't. They asked me to stay in their house until they returned and while I would love to speak to you. I don't want to offend them and not do as they ask."

The woman grinned at her. "All right. I will come to your house, but I can't stay long as my baby is sleeping and I don't want him to wake up before I get home."

Catriona didn't know if they would be happy that she had invited one of the wives to come to their home, but she had so many questions she wanted answers to and yet, she doubted they would ever be interested in marrying her.

They walked into the house and Emma glanced around. "This is very nice. Both of your men are so good with helping out in town and Keegan is great with the children."

"Please have a seat," Catriona told her like this was her home and she was the grand lady. But she was nothing more than a single woman who had over-stepped her bounds by coming to the men to help her.

"Do you mind if I ask you some questions?"

"Oh no, go right ahead."

"What's it like being married to two men? I asked Georgia when we were standing outside and she seemed so happy."

The woman smiled. "Our life is very rich here in Bridgewater. Our husbands take good care of us and make certain we're happy. Yes, they're demanding men, but you will not find better quality of men anywhere. They're honest, dependable and men of their word. I never thought I could be so lucky."

Was it really true? Could this be a place where she could live and be happy? But who was she kidding? Keegan and Alastair had not shown any interest in her.

She sighed. "It sounds so wonderful."

"It is," Emma said. "Are you going to marry Keegan and Alastair?"

How much did she share with this woman? With a sigh, she needed to unburden herself. "Both men are so very handsome and I would marry either one of them. But Alastair hates me. He thinks I'm not pure enough for him."

The woman's brows drew together and she nodded. "He needs the healing touch of a woman. Be patient with him and show him nothing but love. He suffered a tragic loss, and if you marry him, you will need to make certain that he gains your trust."

Just that little bit of information helped her to understand Alastair more.

"So he suffered a loss and Keegan loves children. They seem like such good men and I would love to marry them, but I don't think they're interested in me."

The woman laughed. "Give it time. If it's meant to be, you'll soon be their wife."

Or in jail.

Catriona smiled at the woman. "Thank you. I'm amazed at your town."

"My dear husbands have made this town into a special place. I best be going; my baby will be awakening any moment now." Emma stood and smiled at her. "I wish you the very best and hope that I'll see you again soon."

"Me too," Catriona said as she walked her to the door.

Once she left, Catriona looked around the house. If she married the two men, this would be their home. What would she do with O'Reilly's Folly?

First they had to offer her marriage.

8

*L*ater that afternoon, Keegan had little James sitting in front of him on his horse as they returned to Bridgewater. The day had been terrifying and brought back so many painful memories of the orphanage.

Children often disappeared from the old building in Edinburgh and you didn't know if they left on purpose or wandered off unattended. Sometimes their bodies would be found and sometimes they were never seen again.

It was a heart wrenching memory that he'd tried to forget until today. Today, little James had brought back the horror of those years. The terror of searching the city streets, looking for the lost ones, the fear of finding nothing but a body.

This morning, he feared they would never find the

boy or when they did, he would be dead. But by the grace of God, they had found him asleep in a field. He must have tried to follow his father and once his little legs tired, he'd lay down to nap.

Because James and Keegan had been friends since he was a baby, the men had him ride with Keegan to make the child feel more at ease. The feel of his soft body against his own filled Keegan's heart with love for the toddler.

The child was special and he'd feared the worst this morning. But thankfully, his mother would be delighted when they returned.

As they rode into Bridgewater, the women and the men left behind came flying out of their homes. James's mother came running, crying his name, and Keegan slid off his horse and handed the child to Mattie.

"Thank you," she cried, holding her son close to her chest, sobbing. "Thank you, Keegan."

Oh, how he wished his mother had loved him like this. An ache, an emptiness, opened inside his chest.

"It was all of us," he said, his eyes filling with tears. "We're Bridgewater men and we don't let anything happen to the people we love."

She hugged him to her, keeping James between them. "You're his guardian angel."

No, Keegan was no angel. Only a victim of once being lost himself. The memory of standing on the street corner, crying for his mother returned and slammed into his chest like a bullet.

A sigh came from his right and he glanced over to see Catriona standing there watching. Tears streamed down her face and she hurriedly turned and walked back into their home.

What would make her cry? The child was safe and yet Keegan had teared up when he watched the mother and son reunion.

As the people began to disperse, Keegan pulled his horse to the barn with Alastair following behind him.

"It's too late to take her back to Helena today," he said.

"Aye, it is," he said. "I'm worn out from the hunt. I would just like to sit in front of a fire and rest."

It was what he liked to do when he had a rough day. All the memories that had come flooding back had wrecked his soul. And the fear of having to tell the child's mother that he was dead had sat on his heart like an anchor while they searched.

Thank goodness they had returned the child to his rightful home.

"Maybe we should have her stay with one of the other couples, so she can't claim we took her and insist on her marrying us."

Very seldom did he get irritated with his best friend and brother, but right now, he was ready to punch him.

"Did she do that last night?"

"No," Alastair said.

"Why are you so afraid of this woman? Are you scared that you're going to care for her and your heart will become entangled? When was the last time you fell in love?"

Alastair uncinched his saddle and slid it off the horse. "Never."

"And why is that?" Keegan asked, knowing now exactly why they had not found a wife. His brother was afraid of giving his heart to a woman. So therefore there was always something wrong with every woman they met. And this would happen for the rest of his days.

"The right woman has not come along," he said, not looking at Keegan.

The right woman had not come along because Alastair would never find someone to love if Keegan didn't force the issue.

"We'll take her back in the morning," he said and began to rub down his horse.

Twenty minutes later, they walked into the house and the smell of something delicious filled the air.

"Dinner is ready," she called. "Wash up and then we can eat."

Keegan suddenly knew what he wanted to do. He'd waited too long as it was and with today's realizations, he decided it was time to make a move.

In two big strides, he stood before Catriona who

stood by the stove with a spoon in her hand. She glanced up at him quizzically. "What's wrong?"

"Nothing. It's what I've wanted to do for days and I'm not waiting any longer."

He leaned down, his mouth covering hers. At first, she tensed as his lips wound their way over hers, nipping the edges, his hands brought her mouth in line and he held her there while he devoured her lips.

She tasted of something sweet and he loved the way she seemed to sigh into his body.

Slowly she relaxed and wound her arms around his neck. He pressed his body into hers and she melted into him.

Alastair would consider them being indecent, but he didn't care. He'd waited long enough and today she'd been thoughtful and kind and did her best to make him feel better. As much as he cared about his brother, this was what he'd wanted all day long.

A loving woman waiting for them at home.

Alastair cleared his throat.

Slowly Keegan ended the kiss and she gazed at him stunned. The woman was not an experienced kisser. If she'd never kissed, how could she be pregnant?

"The potatoes are boiling over," he said.

That wasn't the only thing boiling over. Keegan felt like his dick was going to explode at any moment. And yet he knew he had to wait and do what he and Alastair had agreed upon.

"Wash your hands and we'll sit down to dinner," she said, turning away from looking at either of them.

With her back to them, she said, "We're still not having sex tonight."

"Agreed," Alastair said.

"Agreed," Keegan said. "But I couldn't wait a moment longer to taste you. And it was well worth the wait."

Catriona giggled and then turned to put the food on the table.

"Keegan, you are my first kiss."

Glancing at her, he grinned. He knew it. If he was her first kiss, then she was still as virginal as they come.

Alastair was wrong about Catriona. Dead wrong. Now, if only she hadn't killed Phillip.

9

*R*iding into Helena the next day, Catriona's stomach roiled with uneasiness. The last two days staying with Keegan and Alastair had been peaceful. She enjoyed laughing with them, cooking for them, and meeting the people of Bridgewater. But now it was time to face the consequences of her actions.

Time to face the sheriff and admit to her crime.

She could be looking at time in jail for murdering Phillip and yet, she hadn't meant to kill him. If only he would have left her alone, but no, the man was intent on ruining her and now she felt like she was riding toward the hangman's noose.

Murderers in the town of Helena were hung. It was a spectacle. An event the whole town attended.

All she could do was hold her head high and

defend her honor. She'd been a woman protecting her virtue.

As they rode through town, the women turned up their noses and looked the other way. Phillip had done enough damage to her reputation that she would never be accepted again. And she'd done nothing wrong.

That's what irked her the most.

They pulled up in front of the sheriff's office and he came out on the steps.

"Been looking for you," he said. "You're under arrest."

"For what?" Keegan said. "We brought her here to give you her side of the story."

"For attempted murder," he said.

"He's still alive," she said, her eyes widening.

"Yes," the sheriff replied. "He's got a gash in the back of his head, but he's still breathing."

"Thank the Lord," she said with a sigh as she slid off her horse. "I've been so scared that I killed him."

As much as she disliked Phillip, she would never want to kill someone. Not even the man who forced himself on her.

"Come inside," the sheriff said.

The three of them walked up the steps, the two men on either side. Between them, she felt protected and safe.

Inside, she could see the jail cells and wondered if

this would be her next home. Would she soon be looking out from between the bars?

As she sat in a wooden chair, the sheriff took a seat behind his desk and Keegan and Alastair pulled up chairs next to her.

"Tell me why you tried to kill him," the sheriff said, staring at her with dark beady eyes.

"I didn't try to kill him. When I left the barn dance, he was waiting for me. He wanted to ruin me so that I would be forced to marry him and I wasn't having any of it. He covered my mouth so I couldn't scream and then he began to beat me about the shoulders and arms, trying to subdue me, because I was fighting him as hard as I could."

The terror that filled her at the memory had her shaking.

"As a little girl, my papa taught me how to defend myself and that night I pulled back Phillip's thumb so he would release me. I heard the bone snap and he screamed in the night. I pushed him with all my might to get away from him and that's when he fell and his head struck the rock."

She licked her lips and squeezed her eyes tightly to keep the tears from falling. That night was not going to defeat her.

"When I saw the blood spurting from his head, I feared I'd killed him and I ran."

The sheriff sighed. "Are you pregnant with his

child."

Gosh darn it, that just made her mad. She was so sick of fighting this lie.

"I've never slept with him, so how could I be pregnant? I've never slept with any man, but he's been spreading this nonsense around town."

The big man's stomach shook with laughter. "Kind of hard to be with child if you've never even done the deed. But that's not what he's telling everyone."

"And just why do you think he wants everyone to believe that lie? He wants my land. He wants O'Reilly's Folly to be joined with his spread and I would rather see it burn than be given to him."

The sheriff leaned back and considered what she'd told him.

"Sheriff, I know that Catriona's parents died in a blizzard. But if you've lived in Montana for any length of time, you know the signs and when to stay home. Do you know anything about their deaths?"

Shock rippled through her. As much as she despised her father for his actions, she'd always believed her parents died in a blizzard because of foul play. Her father may have been a drunk, but he wasn't stupid when it came to Montana weather. Sadly, no one in town wanted to believe her. Not even the sheriff.

"Mr. O'Reilly was known for his drinking binges," the sheriff said. "We just assumed he'd gotten drunk and Mrs. O'Reilly went after him."

Catriona saw Keegan and Alastair exchange a look behind her back. Shame filled her as she realized that everyone in town had known her father was a drunk. Her mother had pretended that it was just their family secret.

After their deaths, she'd broken every whiskey bottle in the house. She hated alcohol and would never put up with a man drinking. Never.

The door to the sheriff's office slammed open and in walked Phillip.

"You bitch," he said, lunging for her.

Keegan stood and grabbed him by the shirt. "You touch her and you're a dead man. I've already seen the bruises you left on her and you'll not be getting near her again."

Warmth filled Catriona as the terror that spiraled through her at Phillip's entrance slowly died. Keegan would protect her.

"Phillip," the sheriff said. "You'll not be barging in here to cause trouble or you'll find yourself in one of those cells. Pick one out or sit down."

The dark-haired man sank down in a chair closer to the sheriff, blocking the door. If Keegan and Alastair weren't here, she worried that she might have been in even more trouble.

"Arrest her," he demanded. "She tried to kill me."

"I did not," she insisted. "No, I was protecting myself

from his unwanted advances. I want nothing to do with him and he has done everything he could to ruin my reputation. He doesn't want me, but he wants O'Reilly's Folly."

The man growled at her. "Your ranch isn't worth anything. Your worthless father drank all the profits and you're just trying to hang onto the land."

Catriona swallowed the tears that flooded her throat. It was true. Her father had drunk all the profits, but that didn't mean she wanted to lose her family home. What would happen to Charley? The old man was more of a father to her than her own.

"Yes, my father drank too much, but someone is stealing our cattle," she said. "Charley and I are doing our best to keep the ranch going."

"More and more ranchers are reporting missing cattle. Two deputies are trying to locate the rustlers."

At least she wasn't the only ranch missing cattle. But she hated admitting her situation in front of everyone. She hated the pitying looks she saw from Keegan and Alastair. And she hated the gleeful hate reflected in Phillip's gaze.

But more importantly, how did Phillip know they were in dire straits? Who told him the ranch was barely hanging on?

"No one knew about the financial difficulties regarding the ranch except me and Charley. How did you know?"

The man fidgeted nervously in his chair. "Your father told me."

"And when would he have confided in you? He's been dead now for eight months. Our real problems began when the cattle started to disappear and our spring round up found us several hundred head short. Did Papa tell you from the grave?"

Something wasn't right and she just hadn't put her finger on what it was. Charley and she were very tight with information about what was going on at the ranch. The only other person who could possibly have any inkling about what was happening was the banker Mr. Nelson.

"Sheriff, why haven't you arrested her? She tried to kill me."

The portly man turned and glared at Phillip.

"Sounds to me like she's raised some interesting questions and you were the one who attacked her. Even now, I can see the bruises she described fading on her neck and shoulders."

The lawman glanced between the two of them. "Miss O'Reilly, I apologize, but I can't remember the date that your parents died in the blizzard. Could you remind me?"

"January seventh. Momma and Papa went into town to pick up some supplies. When they were found, I thought it was strange that the wagon was empty. Mr. Dierck said they never came into the mercantile. Papa's cash was gone and momma's reticule was empty."

No one had believed her when she said something was afoul. Not even the sheriff. They all assumed her father, the drunk had taken a wrong turn in the snow and they had gotten lost, wandering about until they died of the exposure. But her papa knew the way between town and the ranch. And the team of horses would have found the barn.

They had disappeared.

The sheriff glanced between the two of them. "I don't know what to think. Your thumb is obviously broken, so I know Miss O'Reilly fought you, Phillip. You do seem to be trying to force her into marriage."

Could it be the sheriff believed her?

"She's expecting my child, that's what I'm supposed to do," he said, exasperated. His performance was quite believable and a trickle of alarm scurried down Catriona's spine.

Glaring at Phillip, she hissed. "Stop telling that lie. I would never let you touch me."

A smirk spread across his face. "Darling, you were drunk just like your father when I had my way with you."

For a moment, she thought she was going to either throw up or attack him. How dare he spread lies that she was like her father. Tears of frustration welled in her eyes and she blinked them away.

"That's not true," she said. "There's not a drop of liquor in my home and never will be."

"Stop," the sheriff said. "This is getting us nowhere. Phillip, I don't believe she meant to kill you. You're just lucky to still be alive."

The man gasped. "You're not going to arrest her."

"No, and I want you to stop spreading the lies about Miss O'Reilly. Leave her alone."

Phillip jumped up and rushed her. Keegan grabbed him. "Do not touch her. We're done here. Do you understand me?"

The man leaned around Keegan. "We're not finished. You're going to be mine, one way or the other. And O'Reilly's Folly will also be mine."

Alastair stood and blocked his view of Catriona who sat there stunned at the hatred in the man's eyes. If he could reach her, he would do her harm right here in the sheriff's office.

"This is not over," Phillip screamed as he pulled away from Keegan and stormed out the door.

Catriona put her face in her hands. "What did I do to deserve this?"

Keegan kneeled beside her. "Nothing. He's a very desperate man who will do anything to get your property."

"Miss O'Reilly, I think you're in danger," the sheriff said. "I know your foreman is out at the ranch, but I think you need some extra protection."

Taking her hand, Keegan stood and helped her to her feet. "Thank you, Sheriff. Miss O'Reilly will be well protected. Alastair and I will make certain of it."

The man's eyes glinted and then he nodded. "You men from Bridgewater are well known for taking good care of your women. But I don't trust that Phillip won't try something, so just be on the lookout."

"We will, sir," Alastair said as they hurried out the door.

Once they were outside, Catriona took a deep breath. She wasn't a murderer, but she had a mortal enemy who would do everything he could to make her life miserable. Oh, yes, she was in danger.

Keegan pulled her around to face him. "Catriona, you're in serious jeopardy You need our protection. Marry me and become my wife. We could have a good life together."

Warmth spread through her and yet disappointment filled her as well. She wanted a man to promise her the moon and the stars and forever. Instead he was offering her his protection. And while that was important, she wanted more.

Tears welled in her eyes. "I'm sorry if I don't seem more appreciative and happier. But I wanted a man to court me. To show me he loves me and fill me with happiness." She took a deep breath. "You're certain you want me, the most scandalous woman in town as your wife?"

"Yes," Keegan said.

With a sigh, Alastair stared at her. "You do realize what you're getting into? You will be both of our wives."

She looked between them and thought about the women she met in Bridgewater. No, she didn't love these men, but hopefully with time, she would come to love them and they would her.

"Yes, Alastair, I understand. You'll both be my husband. But do you want me?"

"Oh, I can't wait to take you," he said with a breathless smile. "Just promise me you will never bring scandal on our family."

It was a weird request, but one that given her reputation, she guessed she understood why he was asking for her vow.

"Never," she said as she wiped tears from her eyes. "Yes, I'll marry both of you."

Keegan smiled. "Good. You'll be my legal wife and Alastair's promised wife. We'll take good care of you."

The men were sweet, but she wanted love. She wanted to be courted and showered with promises of love. Instead she would be married to two men for protection.

"Let's go find a preacher," she said, knowing she didn't sound excited, but trying to be happy that at least she had someone who would guard her.

$\mathcal{A}$lastair knew that no matter what, they had to marry Catriona to save her from Phillip. As much as he didn't want a scandalous woman, he would soon be pledged to protect and honor and support one until the day he died. And as much as he didn't like the idea, he couldn't wait to shove his cock into her.

For days now, the woman had tempted him, but he'd refrained. Keegan was certain of her innocence, but Alastair wasn't so sure. The woman could be lying.

Tonight, they would know whether or not she was as pure as she claimed or if she could possibly be carrying Phillip's child. And the revelations today about her papa filled him with mixed emotions.

An alcoholic. A man consumed by whiskey.

He understood what it was like to have a parent who was a disgrace and brought humiliation upon the family. But even that was something obviously the whole town knew about. One more disgrace attached to his name.

Would his name ever be cleared?

All he wanted in a wife was someone who was innocent and came to him without all the shame. He wanted someone who was pure, but even if he found that dream woman, would she be without some skeleton in her closet?

With a sigh, he stood in the church with his friend and Catriona, ready to be the witness to their vows.

The preacher had seemed shocked when they showed up at his door. "Miss O'Reilly are you certain this is what you want to do? Rumors say…"

"Pastor, do you believe in gossip?"

"Of course not," he said.

"Then stop believing it about me. I'm not pregnant with any man's child unless there was a second immaculate conception and I don't believe that is ever going to happen again."

The man jerked back. "Miss O'Reilly, watch what you say."

"Then don't believe lies you've heard," she said. "I'm marrying Keegan Black."

The man sighed and cleared his throat. "If you're determined, then let's do this ceremony, so I can eat my supper."

Alastair shook his head. It was obvious the man

thought Catriona was crazy for marrying them, but he didn't care. If there had been no scandal attached to the woman's name, he would have shoved Keegan out of the way to marry her. Her auburn hair lay in waves down her back, her emerald eyes and dark lashes, full lips, and a mouth made for kissing.

A sweet, sassy mouth that he longed to tame.

Keegan had been the smart one to taste her last night, but tonight, Alastair knew he would get the opportunity and he couldn't wait.

After they signed the paperwork to make their marriage legal, Keegan, who was clearly smitten with the girl and Catriona who seemed sad stood before the preacher and said their vows.

Now she was theirs and while he knew Keegan was excited, Alastair almost felt trapped. Yet his dick was hard and he couldn't wait for the wedding night.

Only question. Did Catriona realize what she had gotten herself into with not one husband, but two?

Once again, Keegan's lips moved over Catriona's and Alastair felt jealous. He should have kissed her before now. When they broke apart, the two of them smiled at each other.

The pastor stood shaking his head.

"Miss O'Reilly, I sincerely hope you know what you've done by marrying this gentleman and that Mr. Johnson knows of your marriage," the preacher said.

"Tell him," Keegan said. "Please shout it in the

streets so he knows she's no longer available. He can no longer harm her."

Catriona glared at the man. "Why would you be so protective of a man who has done everything in his power to ruin my reputation. Twice today, Keegan protected me from him. Pastor, I'm safer now because of my marriage to Keegan. Be happy for me."

The man sighed and they turned and walked out of the church. Alastair fell into step behind them. One thing about their new wife, she wasn't afraid to speak her mind and he kind of liked that about her.

If only the rumors about her were indeed false and she was an innocent like she claimed.

Once they were outside, Keegan helped Catriona on her horse. Together, the three of them rode out of Helena. As far as Alastair was concerned, they didn't have to come back here anytime soon, though he knew that Catriona would need to let the banks know of her marriage and also deal with her family home.

The ranch that butted up against their own land.

The late afternoon sun was sliding toward the horizon as the three of them rode toward Bridgewater. It had been an eventful day and they had an exciting evening ahead of them.

Though he had tried his best not to think of the lovely Mrs. O'Reilly Black, now she was theirs and he couldn't wait to undress her. Touch her lovely skin, slide his cock deep into her willing pussy.

When they were out of town, Keegan pulled his horse to a stop and Catriona followed suit.

"Why are we stopping?"

"Lass, you're first exercise in learning to obey us," he said as he stepped down off his horse and walked to her side.

Taking her hand, he helped her alight, curiosity shining from her beautiful emerald eyes.

"Remove your bloomers," he told her.

"Why?"

"Because I told you too," he said gently. "As your husband, you are to obey me."

"All right, but I don't understand the need."

She pulled her bloomers down over her legs and then her boots. Keegan took the garment from her and raised it to his nose.

"Ah, the sweet smell of pussy," he said as he took a second sniff and then handed the garment to Alastair.

A smile crossed Alastair's face as he inhaled the fragrance.

"Do all men do this? I don't understand," she said.

They grinned at her. Maybe she was an innocent after all.

"Yes," Alastair said. "The smell of a woman's privates is like an aphrodisiac to men. You'll soon see why."

Keegan helped her back up on her horse and they continued on their way to Bridgewater.

An hour later, they rode into town and the men gave them a curious gaze. Tomorrow Alastair would tell Ian and Whitmore of their marriage, but tonight, they wanted their bride all to themselves.

"I'll put the horses up," Keegan said when they reached the house on the edge of town. "You take care of our wife."

Alastair slid off his horse and then turned to help Catriona alight.

She squealed when he lifted her into his arms and carried her toward their home.

"I wanted to feel you in my arms and to carry you over the threshold," he said, his voice rough sounding as he opened the door and took her inside.

He let her body slide down the front of him, her legs caressing his hard cock that was ready to burst with need.

"Oh," she said as she stared into his eyes.

The time had long since passed for him to kiss her, and eagerly, he pulled her head to his lips and slanted his mouth over hers. She tasted of sweetness and honey, and when he pressed her, she opened her mouth and his tongue slid in to command her compliance. Her fingers stroked his jaw and then her hands were around his neck caressing the hairs.

The door flew open and Keegan walked in. "Couldn't even wait until I put the horses up to start?"

Alastair broke the kiss and gazed into her emerald

eyes. "Nay, you've tasted her twice and I've not had her even once."

Kissing Catriona was like a sweet, rich dessert that he wanted more of and Alastair knew he would enjoy taking her tonight. No matter what her status, he would enjoy spreading her legs and plunging his cock deep into her.

Catriona glanced between the two men and Alastair could see she was nervous. The last two nights she'd stayed here, they had not touched her, but tonight would be all about their fingers and their cocks sliding inside her making her a woman, if she wasn't already.

"Sit down, Catriona, we need to talk," Keegan said.

Sinking down on the couch, she gazed between the two men.

"We are your husbands. And you will obey us. If you don't, we will punish you, but we will never harm you. Do you understand the difference?"

"No," she said suddenly looking terrified.

"Tonight on the trail, I told you to remove your bloomers and you did. But if you had refused, I would have pulled you over my lap and spanked you," Keegan said.

"And I will do the same," Alastair replied. "Our job as your husbands is to protect you, keep you safe, and make sure you lack for nothing. We are here to make you happy," he said. "And we will expect the same from you."

"Why would you spank me?"

"Because we're your husbands," they replied.

"But you'll never hurt me?"

"Never," they both replied at once.

"Doesn't a spanking hurt?"

"You'll see," said Keegan. "It can be painful, but it can also be pleasurable."

"I don't understand," she said, frowning.

Keegan grinned and Alastair knew he believed her to be an innocent and so far she sounded like one. "You'll understand after tonight."

"Keegan is your legal husband, but as I stood beside the two of you tonight, I was also reciting the vows. I'm just as much your husband as Keegan. And if you cheat on me, there will be hell to pay."

A frown marred her forehead. "As your wife, I will never cheat on you."

The words were easily spoken, but could she keep her vows?

For a moment, she sat there contemplating what they had told her.

"How do I have sex with both of you? Do we do it at the same time or one at a time? I've been wondering about this all afternoon."

Alastair almost wanted to laugh, but yet again, this made her sound like an innocent. Like she knew nothing about sex with a man and yet Phillip made it sound like he had taken her.

Keegan glanced at him and gave him a smile. It was like he was saying *I told you so*. But the evidence would be there later. And Alastair was determined he would take her first.

"For now, we will take you separately. First Alastair and then me, but later after we've trained you, we will take you at the same time," Keegan said.

"How?" she said, her eyes wide like she had no idea what they were talking about.

"In the morning, we will start to train your ass. Every day, we will change and put a different butt plug in to stretch you. When we are certain you're ready, we'll take you both at once."

He could see that she was growing more and more nervous. "What if I don't like having sex. What if I decide this is not what I want?"

"Then we have not done our jobs as your husbands," Alastair told her. "It's our job to give you pleasure. To make you want to have sex with us to make you come."

Her brows frowned and she shook her head.

"I don't understand," she said.

"Then it's time we showed you," Keegan replied. "Up the stairs. From now on, we will share the bedroom upstairs. Undress and wait for us."

Alastair watched as she took a deep breath, stood,

and walked up the stairs. Already his dick was hard as a rock and he couldn't wait to get up there and claim their bride.

He glanced at Keegan. "I'm taking her first. I'm going to be the man who learns if she is truly a virgin."

A grin spread across Keegan's lips. "Go right ahead, but I'm telling you she's an innocent. And when you realize you were wrong, it's time for you to put your issues with scandal behind you. It's time we showed the people of Helena that she's a virtuous woman who has been ruined by that monster, Phillip."

Keegan was right. Alastair knew he was being difficult, but the misery of his life before he left for the war had left him hurting. And he didn't trust most people and especially not women.

11

___

The day had been overwhelming and tonight she didn't know what to expect. Keegan and Alastair were handsome men, who when they kissed her, her stomach seemed to suddenly have butterflies flying around.

Keegan was protective and intense and after watching him with the child, her heart had melted. The man made her feel special and he said he would kill to protect her. Alastair was more remote and withdrawn and she had yet to understand why he wanted to believe the worst about her. And yet she felt drawn to him like she wanted him to love her for her. In spite of all the drama surrounding her, she wanted him to accept, and yes, love her for who she was.

No, she didn't love these men and that was her

greatest disappointment. Was it wrong to have wanted her husband to court her, for them to fall in love and even get down on one knee and ask for her hand in marriage?

Instead, she'd been proposed to in the middle of the street and it had been more of a *marry us and we'll protect you*, rather than give her the love she so desperately wanted.

A tear trickled down her cheek. Quickly she wiped the tear away. It was done and she was safe.

And now, tonight on their wedding night, she was supposed to remove her clothes and let her husbands take her. All she knew about the sex act was what she'd seen in the barnyard. The horses and the cows, and from what she'd seen, it didn't look like it would be any fun.

Yes, she liked it when they kissed her, but how would she feel when they put their dicks in her. And what about children? Before they married, they had not discussed children and how this marriage would affect them.

The memory of Georgia standing beside her, rubbing her belly, her face filled with love, gave her comfort. Would she feel that way about her husbands and babe whenever she became pregnant?

With a sigh, she began to remove her clothes. It would have been nice to have taken a bath. She always dreamed of a big wedding with her papa or even Charley walking her down the aisle, but that didn't happen. She imagined her mother sitting up front crying and the town people staring in awe as she walked toward the man she loved.

A young girl's fantasy crushed by reality.

Glancing around the room, she saw no place for her to hang her dress, so she laid it on a chair along with her chemise and petticoats. Keegan still had her bloomers and she had the feeling she would never see them again.

The sound of their boots climbing the stairs had her scrambling toward the bed. Quickly she yanked back the covers and crawled beneath them, pulling the quilt all the way to her chin.

Shaking, she lay there waiting for them.

The door opened and both men stopped when they saw her.

"Aw, darling, you're not going to need those covers tonight," Keegan said, unbuttoning his shirt and pulling the garment from his pants. He sank down in the chair and began to remove his boots.

Alastair smiled at her. It was one of the few times she'd seen him smile, and for a moment, it was like a breath of sunshine. Maybe he didn't hate her as much as she thought.

He sat on the bed and removed his boots, socks,

and then he undid the buttons on his pants. Rising, he dropped them to the floor and kicked them out of the way. His shirt came next and then his long johns.

When he turned and faced her, she gasped at the size of his penis. His dick jutted out from his body like a spear ready to pierce her. With a glance, she looked at Keegan and he too was naked as the day he was born.

A trickle of desire skittered down her spine and her lungs seemed to seize as the two men grabbed the quilt and yanked it back.

She lay before them, naked and she quickly covered her breasts with her hands and her womanly area.

"No," Keegan said. "Do not ever cover your body from our gaze. It's so beautiful and you belong to us now."

They took her hands and put them on their dicks. She gasped at the rock hardness and yet the spongy softness at the head. With her hands, they began to rub their members.

"This is what you do to us," Alastair admitted, his words surprising her.

"You make us so damn hard," Keegan said. "We'll try to be gentle with you tonight, but we can't wait to get inside you."

She licked her lips and swallowed hard.

"Understand, we eventually will take you everywhere. Your pussy, your mouth and even your ass. But tonight is all about you and making your first time special," Keegan said.

Alastair didn't believe that she was a virgin, but tonight he would learn the truth. Keegan lay down beside her, his mouth covering hers and she leaned into his kiss, enjoying the way his lips demanded her surrender and left her clinging to him. The way his tongue invaded her mouth, ruling her lips and taking her prisoner.

Fire raced through her and an ache began to build inside her that had her all but clinging to Keegan.

A hand skittered up her leg and suddenly she felt a finger delving into her womanly area. She broke the kiss.

"What are you doing?" she gasped.

"I'm preparing you," Alastair said. "It's our job to make you want us, and before the night is over, you're going to be screaming our names."

Highly doubtful, but she couldn't resist his fingers any more than she could Keegan's lips.

The men continued and suddenly Alastair touched her clit and the most delicious sensation skittered up her spine causing her to lift her hips. A moan escaped her and Keegan broke the kiss.

"Keep doing that, Alastair, she likes it," he said.

Keegan began to kiss down her neck, nibbling on the section around her shoulder and she moved her head to give him more access, enjoying the feel of his lips against her flesh.

Suddenly she felt his hand on her breasts as he twisted her nipple and she cried out at the sharp sensation that filled her. Heat encased her and the urge to part her legs had her gasping. "Keegan."

"We're going to make you come. Go with the feelings, Cat," he whispered against her ears. "We want you to scream with pleasure when we take you."

What was this *come*? She didn't understand and yet an insistent tightness seemed to be filling her as Alastair tweaked her clit, his fingers dancing over her folds.

And then she felt his mouth on the juncture between her thighs, creating a fire in her belly she didn't understand.

"Ahh," she cried as she raised her hips to meet his mouth. Her hands reached down to hold his head there as his tongue skimmed across her clit before sinking inside her.

"Alastair," she cried, her head going back and forth.

"Come for me, darlin'," he said.

Suddenly a feeling so intense seemed to rack her limbs and she couldn't hold the screams inside her as she cried out with pleasure. "Alastair, Keegan."

The men chuckled as she tried to crawl away from

his insistent tongue, but he continued to lavish her nub and the pleasure created stars behind her lids. "Ohh…"

Alastair removed his tongue and his hand slapped her pussy, causing pleasure to grab her once again as she tensed and came again.

Slowly she floated back down to earth.

"What happened?"

"You came," Keegan said with a smile. "And soon we'll give you that pleasure again. But this time, Alastair is going to come with you."

Was this why girls whispered about sex? Was this the reason men seemed to enjoy it so much and yet women were kept in the dark?

Maybe this wouldn't be too bad after all.

Once again, Alastair flicked his tongue across her clit and she jumped at the feeling that gripped her center.

"It can happen this fast again?"

Keegan grinned at her. "For a woman, yes. Not so much for a man."

Why was he the only one responding to her questions? Because Alastair thought she was lying. Pain gripped her chest at the realization that he didn't trust her, but soon he would know the truth.

"Make me a woman," she said, her eyes narrowed on Alastair almost daring him to prove her wrong.

With a nip of his teeth on her clit, pleasure and

pain zinged along her insides. Rising, he lifted her hips and placed his dick at the entrance to her cunny.

Keegan leaned down and whispered, "It will hurt for just a moment when he breaks the membrane."

He believed in her innocence and yet Alastair did not. Staring into his eyes, she all but glared at Alastair, wondering why he had agreed to the marriage when he didn't trust or believe her.

His dick pressed inside her and she knew the moment he felt the membrane as his eyes widened with disbelief and then he thrust, sending pain shooting through her.

She gasped at the pain.

Surprise filled his face and he paused for a moment.

"You were not lying," he said softly.

"No, I wasn't," she hissed, anger filling her at his doubt. "Get on with it. Fuck me."

Slowly he began to shove the rest of his cock into her willing pussy and as much as she wanted to resist, she could feel the pleasure building again. How could she continue to let him fuck her when she felt so angry? How could he not believe her?

"You didn't believe me," she gasped. "And now you're my first."

He slammed into her and she cried out. Over and over again, he pounded her pussy while Keegan tweaked her nipples and layered his mouth over hers. Probably to shut her up.

She closed her eyes, letting the delicious feelings overcome her and suddenly felt a slap to her bottom.

Her eyes opened wide.

"Don't close your eyes. I want to see those emeralds staring at me when you come."

"You want to see my anger flashing at you?" she gasped.

He slapped her on her ass and she glared at him.

A grin spread across his face. "Oh no, darling. When you come, your eyes are going to be filled with passion for me. Passion I created in you."

Oh how she wanted to resist, but could feel her body responding, the orgasm swiftly approaching, and though she tried to hold it at bay, there was no stopping the feelings. He reached down and tweaked her clit and she clenched his cock.

"I'm going to stick my finger in your ass, and when I do, you're going to come all over my cock."

"No," she gasped.

"God, I love it when you resist," he said as his finger tweaked her clit and then she felt him sliding over the skin between her ass and her cunt. "It makes me more determined."

Anticipation filled her as suddenly he shoved his finger inside her.

She cried as the orgasm overwhelmed her, pleasure

filling her as she gripped his cock as he shuddered his release, filling her with his come.

As he slumped over her body, she wanted to push him off, tears filling her eyes.

"You believed the lies," she hissed.

"Yes, I did," he gasped as he rolled them to their side. "Someday I'll tell you why. But I was wrong. I'm sorry."

She felt Keegan slide in behind her and the two men held her as tears flowed down her cheeks.

"Darling, did you not enjoy what you just experienced," Keegan asked.

"Yes, but as my husbands, you're to believe me, trust me and know that I will always tell you the truth," she said.

"You're right," Alastair said softly. "I let my past affect my conscience. I will explain to you, but tonight, please don't cry. It's our wedding night."

He reached up and wiped the tears from her cheeks. "We want you to be happy. We want to pleasure you."

She sniffed. "You did."

Reaching over, he kissed her on the lips. "You gave me so much pleasure. I can't wait to fuck you again."

She sniffed. "Me? A virgin?"

He grinned, leaned down and kissed her softly. When their lips came apart, he said, "Yes, my wife.

Resist me again, and I'll paddle that luscious white ass of yours."

"Oh," she said. "Like you did when I closed my eyes?"

"Even harder," he promised.

Catriona felt a small bit of hope. Maybe Alastair didn't hate her after all. Obviously the man had secrets he wasn't ready to share with her and that made her even more curious.

Keegan rolled her. "Sorry, lass, but I've waited long enough to claim you. It's my turn."

"We're doing it again?"

"Oh yes," he said. "And maybe even again after this. Tonight is all about pleasure. All about showing you what we like."

Alastair moved to the head of the bed and pulled her onto his lap before he flipped her over. "Time for you to suck my cock."

"What?"

"Just like I sucked your cunny, you're going to suck my cock while Keegan takes you from behind."

She licked her lips nervously, wondering what it would feel like to take his cock between her lips. How would it taste?

"Up on your knees," Keegan said as he caressed her ass. His hand felt good smoothing her cheeks and she quickly got on her knees.

She glanced behind her and Alastair pulled her head around.

"My cock," he said in a demanding tone. "Or you're going to feel my hand smack your ass."

With a lick of her lips, she put her mouth on his cock. It had a salty taste that wasn't bad and she realized she was probably tasting herself on his dick.

"Lick around the head and then shove it deeper in your mouth. Like I do when I fuck your pussy."

Slowly she began to lick him and he leaned back against the headboard.

"That's it. Keep it going," he said.

Keegan was behind her she felt his hand caressing her ass with one hand while his fingers twisted her clit.

She moaned on Alastair's cock and suddenly she felt Keegan slap her on the ass. Warmth spread through her cheeks and she turned to look at him, losing her hold on Alastair's cock.

"Why did you do that?"

"Because I love to see your ass cheeks all pink from my handprint. It felt good, didn't it," he said, leaning over and rubbing her nipples with his fingers.

"Yes," she gasped, realizing that even now, warmth spread through her and he was increasing that feeling with his fingers.

Alastair held his cock to her lips and pushed her head down. "Suck."

She continued to suck him into her mouth. Soon

his hands were on her head as he pulled her head down farther on his cock. "That's it. Make me come, baby."

While she was sucking his cock, Keegan, plunged his dick into her pussy and she groaned around Alastair.

"Oh, yes, that's it," he said. "Suck me hard."

Keegan smacked her ass again and she moaned at the heat that rippled through her body. Over and over, he plunged into her and she gripped him with her muscles wanting him deeper.

Alastair groaned. "I'm going to come and when I do, you swallow every drop."

His words made her nervous. What if she didn't want to swallow his come? What if she didn't like it or she gagged?

Just then, Keegan smacked her ass again and this time he drove deep inside her and she yelled around Alastair's cock as she began to come.

Alastair shoved deep in her mouth and held her there while his come shot down her throat.

When he finished, she slumped on Alastair's chest, screaming her release as Keegan pumped into her one last final thrust.

"That's it, baby," he cried. "Squeeze me tight."

And she did just before she collapsed.

All three of them lay for a moment, letting the feelings subside, their breathing harsh.

Now, Catriona understood. Now she knew why they spoke in whispers about sex to women, because it was such a pleasurable experience.

And she had two husbands to make her happy. She had two men to keep her satisfied.

As she lay sandwiched between them, she sighed with happiness. "When can we do that again?"

Both men laughed.

"Soon, darlin', soon," Keegan replied.

12

*B*efore the sun came over the horizon, Keegan stretched, his hand landed on Catriona and he rolled over, wedging her between them.

"This is how we should wake up every morning," he whispered as he kissed her lips.

A groan resounded from her and she snuggled deeper into his body, but that wasn't what he wanted.

Reaching down, he began to play with her clit and she stirred in his arms. "Keegan."

"Good morning, sweetheart."

Before she could respond, he raised himself over her and shoved his cock into her wet, willing pussy. She wrapped her arms around his neck, and in the light of dawn, she slowly opened her eyes.

"Good morning," she said with a sigh. "Oh…"

"Darlin', your pussy is just as tight this morning and what a way to start the day," he said as he leaned down and placed his mouth around her taut nipples.

The walls of her pussy clenched his cock and his fingers played with her clit as he shoved into her.

Last night had been a wonderful night except for when she'd been so angry with Alastair, but he couldn't blame her. The man had not believed her innocence until he took her virginity and then he had no choice but to realize how wrong he'd been.

But Keegan had seen the fear, the desperation in her eyes whenever Phillip came around and he realized the man planned on forcing her to marry him. But not now. Now she was his and Alastair's wife.

"What am I missing out on?" Alastair said, rolling over and facing them.

"Our morning, fuck," Keegan said.

"Roll her over on top of you," he said. "I'm going to prepare her ass."

Keegan rolled them over and she glanced back at Alastair.

"What are you going to do?"

"Focus on Keegan. You'll soon find out," he said as he rubbed her ass cheeks with his hand.

"I think our wife needs to start off the day with a spanking," he said as he slapped her ass.

"Why?"

"Because it makes your pussy wet," Keegan told her. "Do it again."

"Oh," Catriona said.

Keegan felt Alastair shove his finger in her pussy, his cock rubbed the digit, lubricating his finger. Her eyes suddenly widened and he knew that Alastair was playing with her ass. She gasped and tried to look back to see what he was doing.

"Eyes on me, Cat," Keegan said. "Or you won't be coming."

Suddenly, Alastair begin to push in her tight little hole and past the thin wall, Keegan could feel his finger.

"Aargh."

"Someday soon, my cock will replace my finger," Alastair told her.

The feel of his finger, the way the walls of her pussy were clenching his cock, Keegan knew he wouldn't last much longer.

"Are you ready to come?" he asked her.

"Oh, yes," she cried.

"Good, come when I tell you," he said, wondering if she could last that long. With stroke after stroke, he felt his blood building. Alastair smacked her on the ass and she screamed, taking them both over the edge.

With a last thrust, he coated the inside of her pussy with his come. She was his. His and Alastair's and he'd never felt so happy that she had married them.

The sun was up and shining in the window when he crawled off of her and Alastair took his place.

He slapped her on the ass. "Up on your knees. I want to fuck you from behind."

She glanced back at him and narrowed her eyes.

"Nothing is ever simple with you, is it?" she hissed.

A grin spread across his face. "No, and it never will be."

Keegan pulled her up on his lap, her face, even with his cock.

"My turn for you to suck my cock. Wrap your pretty lips around it and suck the head."

Alastair slapped her pussy and she squealed and turned to glare at him.

"That stung," she said.

"Good. Move faster," he said. "I can't wait for your pussy to grip me again."

"Cat, focus on my cock," Keegan said as he watched the two of them and their interaction. It was the first time he'd see a woman stand up to Alastair and he knew these two were going to go at it at for some time.

When her mouth wrapped around the head of his cock, he groaned. "Oh, darlin', that feels so good. Keep sucking it."

Alastair spread her legs, her pussy glinting with moisture in the light.

Shoving two fingers in her, she moaned and raised

her hips to meet his every stroke. Knowing Alastair loved taking her from behind, Keegan lay back and let him do the work on Catriona while she sucked his cock.

"Are you ready for my cock?"

A moan came from her throat.

Alastair plunged into her and she groaned as he slapped her on the ass and pulled her onto his cock.

After last night, it was hard to believe they had been married less than twenty-four hours and yet Catriona was theirs.

Keegan knew he would die protecting his wife and what they shared and Alastair would as well, though he doubted he would admit it. Over and over, he watched as his cock disappeared inside his wife's sweet mouth.

"I'm going to come," he said softly. "Don't waste a drop."

With his cock pulsating, he grabbed Catriona by the head and held her in place as he shoved his member as deep as he could while his come pulsed from his dick.

"Oh," he cried. "What a sweet way to begin the day."

Pulling her head up, he kissed her on the lips and she moaned as Alastair slapped her on the ass again.

"Don't come until I say you can," he commanded. "Or I'll enjoy shoving that butt plug in your ass."

A whimper came from her and Keegan could see she was fighting to keep from coming.

"Now," he said. "We'll come together, now."

One last shove pushed her over the edge and she cried out as Keegan held her in his arms. "That's it," he said, watching her face contort, her emerald eyes darken with passion and her mouth form that perfect circle that made him want to put his cock in there again.

The three of them collapsed on the bed and she took Keegan's hand in hers. "This is not what I expected."

A chuckle came from him and he pulled her in his arms. "Is it better?"

"A thousand times," she said.

Alastair rolled over against her back. "And the best is yet to come."

She glanced back at him and Keegan knew they still did not trust one another. Hopefully, whatever was holding them back would work itself out in the future.

"Time to start your training," Alastair said as he rose from the bed.

"My what?"

"Training," Keegan replied. "We cannot take you both at the same time without training your ass. So this morning, you'll receive your first butt plug."

Her eyes widened with alarm. "What is a butt plug?"

"It will stretch your ass so you can accept our penises," Alastair told her as he lubed up the first plug. "At first, it's going to feel tight and full. But then you will come to accept it."

She licked her lips and Keegan could see she was anxious.

"Honey, it's all about us sharing the pleasure of being together. You're going to love it once we take you at the same time."

Like an innocent child who trusted him, she bit her lip and nodded. "All right."

"Up on your hands and knees," Alastair commanded. "Now lean your head on your arms, with your butt raised in the air."

The man liked to be in charge while Keegan just wanted Catriona to feel special and know how much he was starting to care for her.

"Take a deep breath," he told her as Alastair slapped her on the butt.

Slowly he started to push in the plug and she moaned.

"Loosen up, it will go in easier."

Finally, the wooden dowel was all the way in and they helped her to sit.

"That feels weird," she said. "I don't know if I can do this."

Keegan took her hand and wiped a piece of hair

away from her face. "Of course, you can. Just relax and it will soon feel better."

With a sigh, she sat there watching them.

"For the next three days, we do not want you to wear clothes in the house," Alastair said.

"Why not?"

"We want you ready and available any time we want you. And you are never to wear bloomers again."

Her mouth dropped and she stared at him. "But what if my dress rides up?"

"If your dress rides up, it's because we're taking you from behind," Keegan told her.

Shaking her head, she glanced between them. "What if someone knocks on the door?"

They grinned. "Once we tell everyone we are just married, no one is going to come around until we give the all clear signal. You don't have to worry about visitors."

They sat there staring at one another and then Keegan leaned over and kissed her softly on the lips before he released her mouth. "One other thing. Do not ever go anywhere without letting us know. One of us will always accompany you. You are not to leave the house by yourself. You're in danger."

He could see she was confused or worried. "I want to go to the house and see Charley today. He must be worried sick about me."

Keegan did not want her anywhere near her home for now. Not without one of them being with her.

"We'll send him a message that you're our wife now and we'll be coming to visit soon. But the first week of our marriage will be spent with us staring at your beautiful breasts. Coming up behind you and taking you right then and there or simply enjoying the way your hips sway in the light. You're going to be naked for our pleasure," Alastair said.

"Failure on your part to obey us will get you a well-deserved spanking and not one for pleasure. Or we might tie you to the bed. Your choice."

They were silent as they watched her expressions cross her beautiful face. "Life here is certainly different."

"But it's a good different," Keegan said. "A place filled with pleasure. And as our wife, we intend to make you very happy."

13

___

*L*ater that day, Alastair and Keegan walked out of the house to take care of the animals and to let the other men know they had married. There was a spring in Alastair's step this morning and he couldn't help but grin.

"You were right. She was a virgin and I was completely wrong about her," he admitted.

Keegan glanced at him sideways. "I told you, but you wouldn't listen. You need to get over this obsession you have with disrepute. Maybe it was true about your mother, but it's not true about all women."

Alastair knew what he said was true, but the wound was still there and it still ate at him. As much as he wished it would go away, the pain seemed to recoil and come back stronger when he thought about what they endured.

Even now the thought of Catriona with another man filled him with rage and he feared how he would react.

"I'm glad we married Catriona," Alastair admitted. "At first, I was reluctant, but now, damn man, I love the way she stands up to me. She let me know real quick she knew I didn't believe she was a virgin. No woman has ever stood up to me the way she did. I think it made me like her even more."

Shaking his head, Keegan frowned. "I feared you were going to ruin our wedding night."

"No, and in fact, her defiance made it even better. She didn't like the way I had treated her and she let me know."

Why hadn't his father confronted to his mother, or maybe he did and she still cuckolded him.

"I think the two of you need to talk about your reaction. She doesn't know about your past and you should tell her," Keegan said as their boots crunched on the ground as they walked to the barn.

"Have you told her about your past?"

"No," Keegan admitted with a frown. "When the time comes, I'll tell her, but I wasn't holding over her head my mother's sins. Not like you were."

It was true. He had held his mother's sins over all women he'd met. But this time, the rumor he feared was not true unlike his mother's cheating.

"We need to check to see how the cattle are doing. I

wonder if our friendly rustlers came by last night. You know soon we're going to have to lie in wait for them," Keegan said.

"Yes, I know. But do we have to do it this week when we're training our sweet wife? The very thought of her waiting for us naked and willing is enough to send me running back to the house."

Keegan shook his head at him. "Damn, I never knew you would be a bigger pain in the ass when we married. The woman needs some time alone. She was going to take a bath and freshen up."

A smile crossed Alastair's face. "Fresh pussy. I'm all in. Tonight, we should shave her. Just think about what a bare pussy will taste like."

At the thought, Alastair smiled, his dick already hardening at the vision of her bare, shaved pussy. "I can't wait. You know, Keegan, you were right about everything. I think this could be the perfect woman for us."

Today their plans were to feed the animals and get back to their wife.

"I'm glad you're admitting I was right. Too bad you didn't want her, and believe me, she knows. Catriona is not a dumb woman and she was angry last night because all along you never believed her."

It was true. "I'm going to make it up to her."

He didn't know how, but somehow he needed to confess to her the reason for his reluctance about her.

This first week, they would keep her all to themselves, but after that, he would take her into town and buy her some trinket that he thought would make her happy.

Just as they reached the barn, an arrow whizzed by his head and slammed into the post. A note on the shaft fluttered in the wind.

"What the hell?"

They whirled around ducking low and gazed about the countryside. Several men came running toward them.

"What happened?"

"An arrow landed in the barn door," Keegan told them still glancing around trying to find where the arrow had come from. The urge to jump on his horse and ride after whoever was shooting at them was strong, but by the time he loaded his saddle on the horse, they would be long gone. They had never had trouble with Indians before. Why now?

Ian walked up pulled the message down and then the arrow.

"Not an Indian arrow. This came from someone else."

The man read the note out loud. "You stole what was mine."

Keegan shook his head. "Damn. Phillip Johnson is not going to let this go."

"No, he's not. Save that note. We need to take it to the sheriff."

The men stared at them. Ian asked, "What's going on?"

Keegan stepped forward and grinned. "We married Catriona O'Reilly last night. Phillip thought she should be his."

The men slapped the two of them on the back. "Congratulations. You'll soon be like the rest of us, changing diapers and midnight feedings."

Alastair glanced at Keegan and the man beamed. "I hope so. I'm ready to start our family and give my children all the love they can handle."

This was all he ever wanted and Alastair worried he would rush into marriage just to get a couple of kids. But he had to admit, Keegan had found them a wonderful wife. Soon they would have the family he'd always dreamed of.

As long as the secrets from Alastair's past didn't destroy what they had with Cat.

Just as long as Phillip Johnson didn't destroy what they had created last night with their new wife.

"This Phillip man seems like he wants to cause trouble. We'll need to put extra guards out at night to protect the town."

"Someone is stealing our cattle, so keep an eye out for that as well," Keegan told the men.

The men all slapped them on the back again. "Congratulations. We'll have a celebration after your week-long honeymoon."

The men grinned at them.

"Yes, we would love to introduce her to everyone," Alastair said.

The men dispersed and Keegan walked over to Alastair. "Phillip is going to do his best to either make her a widow or steal her from us. We need to be on the lookout."

"We're the luckiest damn sons of bitches," Alastair said. "The perfect woman wed us and now a man won't give up on making her his. This could get ugly real fast."

Already he could see turmoil in their future and that didn't make him happy.

14

atriona was upstairs when she heard the men come in later that day.

"Wash up," she called. "Dinner is ready."

She had washed all the clothes and hung them outside to dry. While she was outside, she had worn one of Keegan's old shirts and Alastair's trousers. There was no way she was going outside nude.

The dress she had married them in was clean and she put it on. Sure they had told her to remain nude, but they didn't mean while she sat at the dinner table, surely.

This morning she'd taken a bath, washed her hair and freshened up. Tonight she wanted to look good for her husbands. She wanted to look her very best with clothes on.

She'd remembered to leave her bloomers off, and

plus, she didn't have any with her. All of her clothes were back at her home.

Home. She missed her ranch. She missed Charley and knew he would be worried about her.

And yet being married felt right. Last night had been so good. Today, she had tried to do wifely things, like laundry, cooking, and even cleaning the house. Most of the day, she had been without clothes on, but they had not come home until now and surely they didn't want her to cook in the nude.

She walked down the stairs, eager to see her husbands.

When she reached the downstairs area, she found them drying their hands on a towel.

"Hi," she said.

They both turned and glanced at her and frowned.

"You're wearing a dress," Keegan said.

"You disobeyed us," Alastair responded with a frown.

"I did laundry. There was no way I could go outside without my clothes on. Plus, I didn't want to cook in the nude and have grease splash on me."

They both walked over to her and suddenly she feared they were going to tear the dress off her body.

"Wait, I'll remove it."

"Too late," Keegan said.

"If you don't have any clothes, you won't disobey us

again," Alastair said as he ripped the bodice of her dress down.

"Now what am I going to wear," she responded.

"Nothing," Keegan said. "Absolutely nothing. And If I have to hide our clothes from you, I will."

Alastair finished tearing the dress from her body.

"I really liked that dress," she said.

Keegan tore her camisole off. Soon she stood naked before them.

"Are you happy now?" she said exasperated. "You owe me a new dress. You owe me a new camisole and chemise."

"And you'll get one after this week," Alastair said. "But for now, you're to be naked."

A shiver ran through her. This was not what she expected.

"After dinner, you'll also be punished for not obeying," Keegan said. "When we tell you to do something, we mean it."

She placed her hands on her hips and glared at both of them. "I cleaned your house. I did your laundry and I cooked us a good meal and the payback I receive is getting punished? That's not fair."

A smile crossed Alastair's face. "Thank you, but we told you to remain naked and you disobeyed."

"Did you want me to burn myself? Did you want me to hang the laundry on the line, naked? Did you ever conceive that someone might come to the door and I'd be naked?"

The two men glanced at one another.

"Enough," Keegan said.

"You've made your point," Alastair said.

But she just couldn't seem to let it go. It was their first disagreement and she felt certain she was right.

"I wanted to look special for you tonight."

"One more word and you're going to be more severely punished," Keegan said softly. "We heard you and we understand that this situation is new to all of us, but we said to you no clothes the first week. We would have hung the clothes up on the line for you. You can wear an apron while you're cooking, but then you are to remove it. Are you clear now?"

She bit her bottom lip trying to hold back the rage she could feel consuming her. This was not how she had planned this night. This was not what she wanted. But yet, a part of her still wanted to argue.

"Let's eat," she finally said.

The two men glanced at each other and proceeded to go into the kitchen. She had planned on asking them about their lives, their families, and learn about her two husbands, but at this moment, she could feel a pout coming on. They couldn't control her anger and she was filled with it right now.

Once they sat at the table, she put the meal on the table and they glanced at each other again.

"What's wrong now?" she asked.

"Nothing. We're just not use to home-style cooking like this. It smells delicious," Keegan said.

Once she sat at the table, she was shocked when Alastair led a prayer before they dived into the food.

"There's a fresh apple pie in the oven," she said.

Their eyes grew large and she could see they were shocked at what she had cooked.

"Where did you get the apples," Alastair asked.

"There is a tree down the road aways and I went out, in my clothes, and picked them."

A glance between them had the two men frowning.

"Today, while we were walking to the barn, an arrow was shot at us and landed in the barn door with a note attached," Keegan said calmly.

Alastair's face was red. "The note read 'You have taken what's mine.'"

Catriona could feel the blood drain from her face and she knew they were angry that once again she had disobeyed them.

"What if you had run into this man on the road? What if you had been near him and he just decided he would take you. Do you think you could have stopped him?"

She swallowed hard. It had seemed so innocent and she had wanted to make something she knew they would enjoy.

"I didn't think about it," she said.

"We know," Alastair said. "You'll be punished for that as well tonight."

Damn, she was in so much trouble and yet, she had tried to make tonight a good night.

"Maybe I'm not cut out to be anyone's wife," she said.

They laughed. "Oh no, you're not backing out. You'll be a fine wife once we train you. And you learn not to disobey us."

The rest of the meal was eaten in silence and she could feel the tension radiating around the table. Her men were upset with her and yet, she still couldn't see the harm in what she'd done.

Maybe she needed to lay down some rules.

"You have rules for me, maybe I should have rules for the two of you," she said.

The men glanced at each other and she could see they were wondering what to do now.

"Here are just a few things I need. One, if you spank me, don't expect me to give you sex."

The men busted out laughing.

"That's a hard no," Alastair said and she frowned.

"If I cook you a meal that you don't like, you better rave to me how great it is."

They nodded.

"Three I'm not going to do your laundry in the nude. So if you want me naked, don't expect clean underwear that day."

With a smile, they nodded.

"Last, I will never accept either of you hurting me, do you understand?"

Keegan reached across the table and took her hand. "We will never hurt you or harm you in any way, but we will spank you when you disobey. It will sting. But there will never be any bruises on you. We will also spank you to bring you pleasure. To make you come."

Alastair smiled. "If you don't like being spanked for punishment, then don't disobey us," he said. "By the way, this meal is the best I've had in ages. Thank you."

Just like that, he disarmed her. She was ready to continue their battle, but a smile crept on her face.

"Do you like it when we spank you and give you pleasure," Keegan asked. "Don't lie to me."

The memory of what they had done the night before returned and she blushed. "Yes, I like it."

They grinned at her. "Good, because we like spanking you."

"Just don't make me cry. I hate crying," she said softly. "I think I did too much when I was a kid."

The nights of crying herself to sleep after she had heard her parents argue rushed through her and she shuddered. She would never allow that to happen in this house. If they had children and there was a serious argument, it would be had outside and not where the children could hear.

Alastair pushed his plate aside. "Tonight, you're

going to be punished. But not until after we have dessert."

An impish grin spread across her face. "Oh, I'm sorry. When you told me that I was not to leave the house without you and I had picked those apples without you at my side, I decided they weren't good and threw the pie out."

The men looked at each other and shook their heads.

"Dear God, I hope you're kidding or your punishment could be even tougher."

Laughter came from her chest. "Maybe I am or maybe I'm not. You'll have to wait and see."

15

"Go upstairs and wait for us," Keegan told her. "We'll soon be up and you'll receive your punishment."

Alastair watched her ass swaying as she walked up the stairs and couldn't wait to get up there and spank her. The feel of her smooth ass as he slapped her cheeks was something he enjoyed and she had to learn. If she'd been picking apples when the man with the bow and arrow had been there, she could have either been dead or he might have taken her.

The thought terrified Alastair. As much as he had tried to thwart this marriage, now she was theirs and he would defend her with his dying breath.

As he glanced around their home, she had done a wonderful job of cleaning up and the idea of never having to do laundry again was enough to make him celebrate.

"Are you ready?" he asked Keegan.

The man frowned. "I hate punishing her."

"Good, then I'll do it," Alastair said. "I can't wait to make her cheeks rosy."

Keegan shook his head at him. "Obviously, you were never punished much as a child."

"No, I wasn't."

They took the stairs, their boots making a clunking noise.

They walked into the room. Catriona lay naked on the bed. First, her punishment and then he intended to shave her.

Sinking onto the bed, they pulled her up to face them.

"Did we tell you to remain naked," Keegan said.

"Yes," she said meekly.

"Did we tell you to never leave the house without us," Alastair asked.

"Yes," she replied. "But it wasn't far."

"But you were in danger," Keegan said.

"I didn't know," she whispered.

"That's why we want to be with you. We will always accompany you," Alastair replied. "Over my lap."

She bit her lip and he could see that she really wanted to argue more about her punishment and secretly he wanted her to. That would give him even more of a reason to punish her.

"Didn't we tell you that if you disobeyed us, you would be punished," Keegan said.

"I'm sorry. Being married is new to me. I didn't think you were serious."

Keegan's brows rose. "Learn the rules."

"We expect complete obedience," Alastair said, pulling her across his lap.

She bit her lip and gazed at him in a pleading way. "Stop stalling. Now."

Standing, she lay over his lap, her head hanging down, her hair touching the floor. His palm hit her bottom cheeks and not in the playful, sexual way, but in a punishing smack. Warmth spread through his hand.

"Count your licks," Alastair commanded.

"One," she said with a gasp.

Smack, his palm hit her flesh again.

"Two," she said, her voice shaking.

Smack, and this time his hand stung from the force of the blow.

"Three." She moaned, biting her lip.

Smack, the sound reverberated through the room and she cried out.

"Four."

Smack, tears rolled down her face into her hair and she begin to cry. "You said you would never hurt me."

Keegan reached over and massaged her cheeks and it was both torturous and exquisite. The look he gave Alastair let him know that was enough.

"If you don't disobey, then there would be no need to make your punishment hurt. We really only want to give you pleasure, but you have to obey us."

Alastair pulled her up and took her in his arms. "We only want to protect you. Cherish you."

"And keep you safe," Keegan said, wrapping his arms around Catriona.

The bed squeaked as Keegan rose and began to remove his clothing. When he was completely naked, he crawled back in bed and took her in his arms. "We're your men and we're here to take care of you. To fight your battles. Depend on us and let us take care of you."

The bed moved as Alastair rose and undressed. He slipped his fingers between her legs and pulled them apart, his fingers played over her clit. "You're wet. You didn't like the severity of the punishment, but you did like the spanking. We'll spank you with pleasure and for punishment. Do you understand?"

"Yes," she cried out. "But it hurt."

"That's why it's called punishment," Alastair said.

Keegan reached out and wiped tears from her face. "Obey us, Catriona, and you won't have to experience this kind of punishment again."

"I'm trying," she said. "I didn't think it would be such an offense to put on my clothes."

Keegan lay on the bed, his cock rigid, a smile on his face. "Suck my cock."

Reluctantly she crawled over to Keegan and placed her lips around his manhood.

"Now run your tongue around it and suck on the bulb," he said with a moan.

Alastair saw an opportunity as he moved behind her. His fingers teased her clit causing her to tighten around his fingers as they moved over the lips. She moaned and Keegan jerked.

"Dear God, do that again," he said.

Alastair thrust his fingers into her pussy and she moaned. Soon he intended to have her screaming his name with passion. Spreading her cheeks, he put his mouth against her pussy and she moaned.

"The vibration of her moan feels so good," Keegan said.

With his hands, he gripped her hips as he let his tongue work magic on her clit, her pussy lips and even swirling his tongue up inside her. Moisture coated his digits as he prepared to take her.

Keegan grabbed her head and pushed his cock farther in her mouth as he moved her head up and down. Alastair couldn't wait to feel her mouth around his cock.

"I'm going to come in your mouth. Swallow it all,"

he said as he groaned, his body going rigid as he shoved his cock deep in her throat. Unable to wait any longer, Alastair moved behind her. She leaned back, glanced at him, and licked her lips.

Eager to feel his cock constricted, he slammed into her pussy. A groan escaped from her as her body stretched and he filled her with his dick. She moved her hips to accommodate him, and for a moment, they moved in unison as he held her hips, rocking her exactly like he wanted.

But that wasn't all he wanted.

His fingers slid up to her back passage and he tapped the butt plug with his finger before he pulled it out and then shoved it back inside. She gasped.

Alastair moaned. He couldn't wait to get his cock inside that sweet little hole.

"Oh," she cried as he twisted the plug inside her.

"Soon, baby, soon," he moaned. "I'm going to enjoy taking you with Keegan. I'm going to love shoving my big cock up your tight little hole."

Keegan reached for her nipples and twisted them. "Soon you're going to take our cocks at the same time."

His lips covered hers and Alastair could feel his come starting to build as he plunged into her pussy over and over.

She released Keegan's mouth. "I'm going to come."

"Not yet, you're not," Alastair said, and he slapped

her ass, but this time between the two of them, it was more pleasure than pain.

"Alastair," she cried as she bit her lip.

Shoving the plug in her, he twisted it one more time.

"Now, you can come," he said as he slammed his cock into her one last time, his seed spilled against the walls of her pussy.

She screamed with pleasure, her body shaking and undulating as the orgasm rocked her over and over.

Alastair and Catriona collapsed onto the bed. The two men moved her until she was between them.

"This is where you belong," Keegan said as she slowly recovered. "This is how we will always protect you."

"If you disobey us, you will be punished, but we will always keep you safe," Alastair said, gasping for air.

They lay in silence as they all three seemed to catch their breath.

Finally, Keegan stood and walked to a dresser nearby. He opened the drawer and pulled something out and brought it back to her.

"It's time we shaved you," he said.

"Do all married couples do this? I've never heard of the woman wearing a butt plug or being shaved."

Alastair smiled. "Welcome to Bridgewater. We like to live for pleasure. Yours and ours."

With a sigh, she lay down while Keegan prepared a cup full of shaving cream and a razor.

"Spread your legs, darling," Keegan said.

She did and he rubbed the brush between her legs, stroking her lips.

"Oh," she cried.

"What are you doing with the razor?"

"I'm going to make that pussy shine," he said. "No more hair."

"Keegan," she gasped.

"Relax," he told her. "I'll make it good for you. Each time the brush touches you, you'll feel pleasure."

Alastair watched as she gripped the sheets on the bed and tried not to moan. "Oh, Keegan."

In a matter of strokes, Alastair was shocked at the outcome. Her pussy glistened with his seed as the full lips peeked out.

"Now for your second butt plug," Alastair said, rising from the bed.

"Up on your knees," Keegan demanded.

Slowly, she turned over and crawled onto her knees. He pushed her head down until her ass was in the air. Alastair watched as Keegan's fingers stroked her clit and pushed into her pussy.

"Oh, Keegan," she moaned, "make me come."

"Not yet. The best is yet to come," he said and slapped her pussy.

A scream tore from her throat. Not one in pain, but pure pleasure. "Oh, do it again."

And he did.

With his finger, Alastair pushed the lubrication into her ass and then spread her hips, exposing her back passage.

"Get on with it, man. I want to fuck her," Keegan said.

Slowly he pushed the second butt plug in her.

"All in," Alastair said and gave her a smack on the ass.

She yelped, but it sounded more like a moan.

"On your back and spread your legs," Keegan commanded.

Keegan took his time as he pushed into her and she groaned.

"Damn, she feels even tighter," he said as he began to plow into her pussy.

Alastair sank down on the bed and twisted her nipples before he leaned into kiss her, his mouth ravaging hers. He demanded that she surrender under the assault of his lips and she groaned.

She was helpless. They were her masters and she was all theirs to do with as they wished. And Alastair had always liked his sex a little rough. With Catriona, he wanted to push her to the very brink before he soothed the maelstrom he created.

"Oh," she cried into Alastair's mouth as his tongue

ravished her. He broke the kiss and she screamed, "Please, Keegan, let me come."

He raised her legs and over her shoulders as he pounded into her pussy and then he smacked the butt plug.

"Now you can come," he said as he sent vibrations through her again.

The smack was hard enough that even Alastair could feel them through her lips.

"Keegan," she screamed as Alastair gathered her in his arms and she disintegrated.

Alastair stared down at Catriona and knew that if he wasn't careful she could win his heart and his love and that made him extremely nervous. In fact, it frightened the hell out of him.

16

For the next week, they kept her inside and she remained naked. One of them always showed up for lunch and before he left, she would be taken again and again. Lunch was not food, but rather them having sex and she came to enjoy the private time with each one of her husbands.

While this life was not what she expected, it was much better and she found herself waiting for them to walk in the door and have their way with her.

Last night, she'd been lying on the table, naked, her legs spread, her pussy covered with pie and both of them had licked her clean. Tonight, she would be draped over a chair, her ass ready for them to spank her for some minor transgression.

The first week was up today and while she was glad

she could return to wearing clothes, she still planned on greeting them nude.

But she also planned on asking them to take her to her home. She wanted to gather some of her possessions to bring here and talk to Charley to let him know she was happy. What she would do with the ranch, she didn't know. But because of Charley's devotion to her, he would always have a home either there or here in Bridgewater.

The man had helped her since she was a child. He'd comforted her when she was angry, consoled her when her parents were killed and made certain she was safe and protected. In some ways, he'd been a better father than her own. At least she'd never seen him drunk or fighting mad.

A shiver went through her as she walked outside and pushed the memories away of her father. That man could rot in hell as far as she was concerned.

Taking a broom, she began to sweep the porch. Every day, she had taken a room in the house and cleaned it thoroughly. While her husbands were good men, they were not great housekeepers and now she had their little home spotless and even the root cellar she had organized so they knew what items they needed when they went to town. She had started making a list and hoped she could convince them to take her to the mercantile and her own home.

Several of the other ladies were out hanging

clothes on this beautiful fall day. The wind held a nippiness that promised winter would soon be arriving.

With a sigh, she glanced up to see a rider approaching from the east.

The closer he came, the more she recognized his features and fear gripped her. What the hell was Phillip doing riding here?

She glanced around to see if anyone else noticed the rider. But most of the men were out working the cattle, preparing them for the winter, bringing them in closer to the settlement. Her own men were working their cattle and very few men were here in town.

The moment he stopped in front of her, she should have screamed. He glanced around nervously.

"Where are your husbands?"

"In the barn," she lied, hoping he would go away.

He laughed. "No, they're not. It's time to bring the cattle in closer for the winter. They're out riding the range, looking for missing cattle."

She wanted to take the broom and beat him with it but knew he would yank it away from her. How could she protect herself from him?

"You really are a whore," he said, smirking. "Living in this place."

"I'm married, leave me alone," she said. "Go away or the men are going to come see what's wrong."

An evil smile filled his face and his eyes darkened.

"If you want Charley to live, you'll come with me now. I have him and I'll kill him if you don't come with me. Your choice." His leg knocked against the rifle he had attached to his saddle, purposely calling attention to the weapon.

Terror gripped her chest as she stared at the man. There was no way she was going to let Charley die. She glanced around the town and everyone seemed to have disappeared. There was no one to see her leave.

"Let me leave a note for my husband," she said.

"No," Phillip said. "You come right now or I will shoot him when I return."

After everything Charley had done for her, she couldn't walk away from him. All she could hope was that someone would tell Keegan and Alastair and that they would have enough faith in her to know she would never leave on her own accord.

"I don't have a horse," she said.

He grinned. "You're riding in front of me. And I plan on taking advantage of you every moment of the ride. Maybe I'll return you to your husbands with a baby in your belly."

What the hell was she doing? If only she could save Charley some other way. But by the time the men returned, he could be dead. She had no choice but to go with Phillip.

"They will kill you," she said as she put her foot in

the stirrup and crawled up in front of Phillip. "You're a dead man."

He laughed. "Keep believing that. Because I'm going to have an ambush all set up for them. They may come after you, but they'll never live through what I have planned."

Her heart slammed into her chest, aching. Suddenly she realized that she loved her husbands. She loved them with all her heart and soul and if they died trying to save her, she would kill Phillip. He would deserve to die at her hands once and for all.

Tears rolled down her cheeks as she thought of Keegan and how she loved his tender, kind heart and would give anyone the shirt on his back. Especially a child.

She thought of Alastair, who was so cold on the outside, but once he accepted you, was a gentle giant of a man who commanded like a general but had the heart of someone who had been hurt and no longer trusted people. What would he do once he realized she'd been taken?

"Oh, look, you're crying," he said, laughing. "Well, don't worry, you won't be crying for long because I plan on taking you every possible way. Starting right now."

He reached around and pinched her breasts not in a light teasing manner, but one that hurt.

"Is this the only way you can get a woman?"

"Oh, honey, don't worry, you will never be my main

woman. You'll only be with me long enough for me to get what I want from you. Your pussy and your land. Once I've had both, you'll be with your parents."

"So all this time, I was right. All you wanted was my land. The sheriff is aware and you'll never get away with this."

The man laughed a wicked sound.

"You've been away. You haven't heard the news that the sheriff was killed this week? Seems his horse got spooked and dragged him halfway across the county. The man was so beat up that they had to close the casket at his funeral."

Her stomach knotted and it was all she could do to keep from throwing up. She knew she was in real danger and she turned and started screaming. A slam against her head had everything going dark. Her last thoughts were of her love for Keegan and Alastair.

17

*L*ater that evening, Keegan and Alastair returned home just as the sun was setting after a long, tiring day of trying to locate their missing cattle. He loved this time of day and was just sorry they had been unable to get home for lunch. But winter would be arriving any day and they had been rounding up all the cattle and making certain they were close to home. Plus, this way they could thwart the cattle rustlers.

Soon they would be sitting in front of a fire with their lovely wife spread between them. He could hardly wait.

"Wonder what's she's got planned for us tonight," Alastair said with a grin. "Eating pie off her pussy, that was my favorite. Damn, it was still warm from the oven."

Keegan laughed as they rode into the barn. "I don't know, but I can't wait to see. Coming home has never felt quite so good."

For over a week now, they had enjoyed their wife. Sharing her pussy and preparing her ass to soon take her together. Keegan had never dreamed being with Catriona would be so pleasurable.

"Yeah, I agree. Who knew that being married would be so good?"

Suddenly Daniel Hamilton, entered the barn. "Been waiting for you men to get back all day."

Keegan turned and frowned at him.

"What's up?"

He pulled his wife up beside him. "Georgia thinks Catriona might be in trouble."

The woman stood shaking her head. "I'm sorry. I wanted to stop him, but the baby was crying and hanging onto my skirts. She got on a horse with a man and before they got to the edge of town, she was screaming for help and then she went silent. She slumped against him on the horse."

Fear filled Keegan and he knew immediately that Phillip had returned for Catriona, his wife. Quickly the fear turned to anger at the thought of what even now, he was probably doing to Catriona.

"As soon as Daniel and Martin got home, I told them what I saw. At first, she appeared to go willing, but in the end she was fighting him."

"Did the man have dark hair?" Alastair asked.

"Yes," she said. "Do you know him?"

"It sounds like Phillip. He's the man who wanted to force her to marry him. But why would she climb on his horse and go with him?" Alastair asked, eyes narrowed.

"Charley," Keegan said. "She'd do anything to protect that man and Phillip had to know that. He must have told her that he had Charley."

It was bad enough that she went with Phillip, but he knew that she loved Charley and would do anything to protect him. He must have told her something about the older man. Otherwise, he didn't know why she would go so willingly with Phillip. She hated the man.

Daniel frowned and shook his head. "There's something else you need to know. When we were in town yesterday, we learned the sheriff is dead. Said his horse killed him."

The two men looked at each other and stopped taking the saddles off their horses. "We better get going."

"Be careful," Georgia said. "That man looked mean."

"He is," Keegan said, pulling his saddle strap tight again. Fear filled him that they would be walking into a trap. Phillip would want them dead if he was going to marry Catriona.

"Let's ride," Alastair said.

The couple stepped aside as they rode their horses out the barn.

"Good luck," Daniel called.

"Thanks for letting us know," Keegan replied as he kicked the sides of his horse and the two men rode hard toward Helena.

"Phillip's or Catriona's house?" Alastair said.

"Phillip's. They won't expect us there. You know he wants us dead."

"Oh, yes," Alastair said.

For a moment, Keegan tried to put himself in Phillip's position and what he would do. He would take Catriona to his house and place his men at her place. But what would he do with Charley? Because Catriona would expect to see the man alive or she would be hell to live with.

But what if he was wrong? What if they were all gathered at Catriona's? What if Charley was already dead?

Something seemed to smack him between the eyes, he suddenly stopped his horse.

"What's wrong?"

"I'm just thinking out loud here for a moment. What if Charley is behind this? What if Charley is not the good man she thought him to be. Maybe he wanted her to marry Phillip for some reason."

"No," Alastair said with a frown. "What's in it for him?"

Something was eating at him like an ant carrying a heavy load to their queen. Something was warning him about Charley and he didn't understand why.

"Don't know. But he was foreman when her parents were killed. And now that I rethink about the first time we met Catriona, remember he warned us that another man had set his sights on her."

It was like he was warning them away from her, and at the time, it didn't seem obvious.

"True, but the man has been with her for years. She completely trusts him."

And that's what bothered Keegan the most. If she believed in this man, he could do anything he wanted to her property.

"That's what is so devastating. His betrayal would make this the worst thing that ever happened to her. I'm not saying he's the bad guy, but her cattle have been disappearing as well. He would have access to everything. He could take O'Reilly's Folly completely down and leave her destitute."

Alastair stared off in the distance for a moment. "I don't know. What if she went to sleep with Phillip, knowing we wouldn't be home for a while?"

"Good God, Alastair," Keegan replied, disgusted, "get on with your life, man. I'm tired of hearing your disbelief in her." He turned his head and squeezed the reins in his hands, then they pushed their horses, trying to reach Phillip's spread before sunset. They needed a chance to check out his place. To find out if Catriona was with him.

The sun was just beginning to set when they rode up to the fence line of Phillip's ranch. In thirty minutes, it would be dark and then they could approach his home.

"I don't know about you, but I think we should tie the horses up here and sneak up to the house to see what we can see," Alastair said. "I'd have a posse of men waiting for someone to come riding in."

"Agree," Keegan said. "If he kills us then he can marry Catriona."

"Our wife is not going to be made into a widow. Not tonight."

18

*C*atriona awoke when Phillip dropped her on the ground. Her head was pounding as she opened her eyes and tried to focus on the sight before her.

Charley was standing over. "Girl, time for you to wake up."

She glanced up at him and then shook her head. "You're safe. Phillip was threatening to kill you."

In the background, she could hear Phillip laughing and shook her head, confused.

"Told you she didn't know," she heard him say. "You owe me that jug of whiskey."

"Shut up," Charley told the man.

"Are you all right?" Charley asked her.

She gazed at him disoriented. Something wasn't right. It seemed that Charley and Phillip were friends.

They were laughing. Confusion filled her as she shook her head and tried to clear the fuzziness.

"Charley, what are you doing with Phillip?"

He ignored her question. "I need you to sign some paperwork for me."

"What paperwork?" she asked suddenly suspicious. "You know I would do anything for you. But first I need to understand why you're here at Phillip's. He told me he was going to kill you if I didn't come."

Phillip stood behind Charley with a gun in his hand. "And I will if you don't sign over your property to me."

"Don't you think that's going to look suspicious if I sign over my ranch to you and then I'm found dead?"

A grin spread across Phillip's face. "No, because I'm sure even now your husbands are riding to save you at your ranch. There, they will be met with a group of men who will kill them. You see there was a lover's quarrel and Charley here witnessed it. Now all three of you are dead and I have the ranch."

Charley turned and frowned at him. "Not you, we."

Stunned, she looked at him. "Charley, I don't understand. Are you betraying me?"

The man shook his head. "All you had to do was marry Phillip and then none of this would have happened. Your mamma and papa were out of the way and I kept pushing you towards Phillip, but you refused to do what I wanted."

The thought of her mother and father had her heart skipping a beat. "You watched Momma and Papa head to town that morning. You hitched their horses." The realization had her chest aching. "You killed them."

"No, they died in a blizzard because the wheel spoke broke on the wagon."

It was true, but she knew something wasn't right.

A grin spread across his face, and for the first time, she noticed the evil in his dark eyes. "I kind of helped weaken the spoke, but it was only because your father was such an ass. He refused to give me a pay raise. I'd worked for him for ten years and not a penny more. And when I asked him to hire my son, he said no."

"Son? You have a son?"

"Yes, I do," he said.

Stunned, she sat there on the floor staring at the man she'd considered her second father, she couldn't believe she'd been so deceived. "I believed you. I trusted you."

"And that's why you now need to sign the paperwork that gives the ranch to me," Charley told her. "You know nothing about ranch work and this way, my son and I can make it into a profitable ranch."

"No. I'm not signing any paperwork."

"Then, once you're a widow, you get to marry me," Phillip said with a laugh. "After all, we're going to get

O'Reilly's Folly one way or the other. It doesn't matter how."

Confusion rippled through her. "Why are you working with Phillip?"

"Because he's my son," Charley said softly. "All these years, I've had to hide his identity, but not any longer. Once his legal father died, I didn't have to hide the fact that he's my boy."

She felt someone had hit her upside the head with a tree trunk as she stared at the two of them. "This is why you kept pushing me toward him. This way you would have both pieces of property."

"Yes," Charley said.

"If only you would have married me, things would have been easier," Phillip said.

"No way in hell was I going to marry you," she said.

Phillip walked over and yanked her up from the ground. "Now you're mine regardless."

He pulled her up against his body and Charley shook his head. "I'm going to ride over to the house and make sure that she's a widow. You kids have fun."

Catriona glared at him, her heart filling with hatred. She spat in his face and the older man smiled. "You got a touch of your father's spirit in you. It's a shame he hid it in a bottle that I always furnished for him."

Speechless, Catriona remembered her mother

saying she didn't know where her father found the alcohol and now she knew.

"You're a disgrace," she said. "I believed in you. I trusted you and you took advantage of my family. Rot in hell, because if I get a chance, you'll not live to see tomorrow."

The old man smiled. "Cat, you always were bull-headed. But don't worry, once Phillip is done with you, after you're married, you'll be dead."

The man turned and walked away and she stared at him, wishing her eyes were daggers. The man had betrayed her and that made her sick.

"Get undressed now," Phillip demanded. "You're used goods, but I'm still going to enjoy fucking you."

She didn't move, not willing to betray her husbands. She would never willingly give her body to Phillip for any reason. The man was despicable and a shudder of revulsion swept through her.

"No," she said and he backhanded her. Dazed, she realized she'd never been hit by a man before. Sure, her husbands spanked her, but they would never hit her.

Tears welled in her eyes. "I hate you."

"Good, you'll be so much more enjoyable with me knowing how much you hate what I'm doing to you."

She slowly unbuttoned her blouse and removed it. Then her boots and next her skirt. All that covered her was her chemise.

"Oh, nice. No bloomers. Is that so they could fuck you whenever they wanted?"

That was a question she refused to answer. It was none of his business what had gone on with her two loving husbands. Her heart squeezed as she thought of them and how they would feel knowing that Phillip had done this to her.

"About now, you're probably a widow. My men were lying in wait for them. Won't they be surprised as the bullets tear through their flesh. Wonder if their last thoughts will be of you?"

Tears welled in her eyes and she thought of Alastair and Keegan. She sent up a prayer for their safety and hoped they were safe at home in Bridgewater.

Suddenly her spine stiffened. There was no way that she would let Phillip touch her without a fight.

Picking up an empty bottle, she stared at him. "Come near me and I'll kill you with this."

He grinned. "My pleasure."

He advanced toward her and suddenly the window broke and Keegan rushed at them. Phillip's eyes grew wide with fear and Keegan ran to her side and pushed her behind him.

"Come on, little man, show me what you got," he hissed. "You're never touching my woman, do you understand."

Keegan threw the first punch and it smashed Phillip's nose, the cracking sound echoing in the room.

"Son of bitch, you broke my nose," he screamed.

"That's not all I'm going to break," Keegan cried as he stepped toward him and he threw a second punch that hit him in the eye. The man went down to the floor.

"Get up," Keegan yelled.

Where was Alastair? Why wasn't he helping Keegan?

If Charley heard this noise, he would be running to help his son and there was no way Catriona would let him get away with this. She would rather see him hang.

Phillip stood and spit at Keegan who dodged him. "What did you do with Charley?" he asked the man as he avoided his fists.

"He's dead," Phillip said.

"No, he's not," Catriona cried.

"Shut up," Phillip told her.

"He's on his way to my house, to make certain you and Alastair are dead. They planned on ambushing you there."

Keegan grinned at him. "Are you ready to give up?"

"Hell no," he said. "I'm going to kill you right now."

He charged Keegan and hit him in the stomach pushing him at the stove. There was no way that Catriona could let any harm become Keegan. She raised the bottle still in her hand and smashed it over Phillip's head.

"Damn you," she said. "No one hurts my husband."

Keegan let Phillip's body slump to the floor. Then he smiled at her. "Remind me to never let you get angry with me."

She flew into his arms. "Oh, Keegan, I was so frightened. I'm so glad you came after me."

He wrapped his arms around her and held her tightly. "No one steals my woman, my wife from me. No one."

She held onto him like she never wanted to let him go. She loved this man with all her heart and soul.

"Where's Alastair," she asked. "He's not hurt is he?"

She felt Keegan tense in her arms. "He's not hurt physically, but darling, you have to understand that there are things in his past that he has a hard time getting over."

Amazed, she let go of Keegan. "Did he believe I wanted to have sex with Phillip?"

"You need to ask him," Keegan said.

Rage filled her. After everything they had shared, how could he not realize that she would never cheat on him or Keegan? She had even told him she would never cheat on him, but words didn't seem to be enough.

Keegan glanced at her. "Damn, I don't know who I feel sorrier for, Phillip or Alastair. The man doesn't realize how much his actions have hurt you."

It was true. He didn't know. But he would soon

understand exactly how she felt about his absence tonight.

"Take me home, Keegan."

After he tied up Phillip for the sheriff to find, he helped her dress and then he wrapped his arm around her as they walked out of the house. She grabbed the paperwork Charley had wanted her to sign before she left the house.

Maybe they had not been caught yet, but she would soon see them in jail.

When they reached Keegan's horse, he helped her on and then crawled up behind her.

They began the long journey back to Bridgewater. Suddenly Alastair appeared before them with Charley, who sat tied on his horse.

"Look who I found," he said delighted.

Catriona refused to look at the man she had once thought of as her second father. The man she trusted.

"I never want to see him again," she said.

"Well, it seems there is a large herd of cattle not far from here. And guess whose cattle is mixed amongst the herd. Ours, Catriona's, and other families' from Bridgewater. He and Phillip are our cattle rustlers."

Keegan nodded. "Good work. We'll wait for you while you leave him at the house. Both men tied up there and we'll contact the law."

Catriona was exhausted and all she wanted to do was crawl into bed.

"I just want to go home," she said with a moan. She hurt all over from where Phillip had hit her. She was both emotionally and physically tired and she was mad as hell at Alastair.

Things were going to change and she was just the person to make it happen.

It was the middle of the night when they rode into Bridgewater. Several times, Catriona had fallen asleep in Keegan's arms, but she was wide awake now and she was ready to make them realize the harm they had done.

All she'd ever wanted was a man to court her and make her feel like he cared for her and her only. That he would protect her, and while most of the time she felt that way with Alastair, she wasn't certain.

But they both could do better.

Keegan pulled his horse to a halt in front of their home. She slid down and then she turned on both of them.

"Hear me out," she said loudly.

Both men turned to stare at her.

"Tonight, Alastair, I'm very disappointed in you.

You didn't trust me enough to know that I would never cheat on you. Maybe you men have had me way too easy. You didn't have to court me. You didn't even have to woo me into your bed. But no more."

She took a deep breath. "Until you can prove to me that you believe in me, you trust me and think I'm the wife for you, you can sleep in the barn. I'm tired of men taking advantage of me and feel betrayed by the whole lot of you."

"Honey, I rescued you," Keegan said in defense.

"Yes, you did, but even you have been a disappointment. I want a man who loves me, cherishes me and is willing to go through hell for me. I'm tired of being disappointed and you never had to court me. Neither one of you. I've done everything you've asked me to do. What have you done for me?"

"We married you," Keegan said and she knew he didn't understand.

Alastair stood watching her. "Catriona, don't do this."

"Both of you will sleep in the barn tonight. I need some time to think and make certain this marriage is what I want."

With that, she walked into the house and shut and locked the door.

Then she sank down onto the floor and cried. Damn, damn, and double damn. She loved them both with all her heart, but Alastair didn't trust her and believed her an immoral woman.

And Keegan. The man was so very sweet, but she deserved a man who would court her and love her and make certain she was happy. All they wanted her for was to have sex every night.

Didn't she deserve two loving husbands?

"Catriona, let me in," Keegan said softly.

"Go away. Leave me alone tonight. I need some time to figure out what I want."

A deep sigh could be heard on the other side of the door and finally she heard his footsteps walking away. Why could they not show her they loved her. Why could they not appreciate her and give her what she needed?

Tonight the world seemed like a horrible place. A man she trusted completely had betrayed her, killed her parents, and tried to force his son on her. All so they could have her land.

Alastair had not helped save her. And Keegan, bless his heart, while he may love her, he had not said anything. She needed to hear their reassurances. She needed their love.

She removed her clothes that held the stench of Phillip and Charley. Lying naked on the couch, she cried herself to sleep.

20

The hike to the barn had been long and Alastair had never felt more dejected. This was all his fault.

There were two bedrolls stored in the barn and they pulled them out and spread them on the hay. Nothing was said until Keegan turned off the lantern and lay down in the dark.

At first he was silent, but Alastair could feel the tension between them. Finally it seemed to explode from him.

"Damn it, Alastair, she's furious with you and me both. When are you going to put your mother's dealings behind you?"

What could he say? He'd taken one look at her through the window, removing her clothes, and all the hate for his mother came rushing back – all the pain of her adultery and he was certain that somehow Catriona must be cheating on him.

The image of his mother rushed to his mind and he thought he was going to throw up right there. So he'd turned and ran away, like a coward, leaving Keegan to save her.

"You knew Phillip had taken her. She didn't go there of her own free will," Keegan said.

The man didn't understand that he'd walked in on his mother having sex with Mason Cook and it had been her own free will. She'd been enjoying herself and that had scarred him for life. Seeing his mother betraying his father tormented him.

Then when the papers wrote the article about her, he'd been humiliated. But when his father killed himself, that had been the end of their family. He'd walked out the door and never returned. His brothers and sisters had done the same. All of them had gone their separate ways to avoid having to relive the humiliation.

They had never spoken again and he didn't even know where they were.

He'd joined the army and never looked back.

But women. He never trusted women, and even now, he wondered if he ever could. Maybe this time, she hadn't been cheating, but what about the next time? Could he continue this marriage if he feared he would find her in bed with another man?

Just seeing her removing her clothes had shaken him.

"You're right. I was wrong to walk away. Even now, it's all I can do not to run in there and call her an adulteress."

Keegan lay there for a moment in the darkness. "If you do, she will leave us. You've got to get over this or there is no hope for our marriage."

How did one get over the biggest scandal in Scotland? The biggest humiliation of having the papers post photos of their mother and write articles of how she and Mason, a married man, had been having a clandestine affair. Of finding his father dead from his own bullet?

"My father committed suicide after my mother's affair was leaked to the papers," he said. "My family all left town to get away from the sordidness of what happened. I don't even know if my mother is still alive. And I really don't care."

No one understood what it was like to attend school and have the boys call your mother vile names and laugh about her. The pain had been unbearable.

"And that was a terrible thing you had to endure. I can't even imagine. But Catriona is not your mother. She was not having an affair with Phillip. If we had not arrived there in time, I shudder to think what he would have done to her."

As much as he considered Keegan his brother, he didn't understand.

"I saw her undressing before him," Alastair said, his heart wrenching.

"Not because she wanted to," Keegan admonished. "The man intended to rape our wife. I wanted to kill him, but she busted a bottle over his head. You know this shows you don't trust her," Keegan said.

"I know," he said. "I was wrong, and no, I don't want her to give up on us."

"Then you're going to have to do some major groveling. Because she's angry. In fact, I think she's furious at both of us."

For a moment, they were silent as they lay on straw in the darkness of the barn.

"Why would she kick us out of our own home?" Keegan asked.

"We've done our best to make her happy," Alastair said.

As they lay there, Alastair's heart ached. He missed Catriona. He missed the warmth of her arms. Shocked, he suddenly realized the reason it hurt so badly when he saw her undressing was not because of what happened with his mother, but rather he'd fallen in love with her. He loved Catriona and if she cheated on him, he'd be as big a fool as his father.

And yet his heart ached with the pain he'd caused her. He wanted to share his life with her. To grow old together, to have children and a family. He wanted her to understand the pain he'd endured at the hands of his family.

"I really messed up," he admitted in the dark. "I ran. When I found Charley with the stolen cattle, I hoped I would be forgiven. But she doesn't understand."

And yet he knew that was not enough. It would never be enough. Could he give her the trust she needed?

"What if I can't trust her? What if I can't give her the unconditional love she requires?"

Keegan lay there not saying a word. Alastair wondered if he'd fallen asleep.

"We're brothers. As much as I don't want to give up Catriona, I would. But I'm hoping you're going to realize this woman is special. She's different. You need to tell her why you left. Why you couldn't watch another moment. I think she'll be all right once you tell her," Keegan said with a sigh. "At least I hope so."

Alastair stared in the darkness. "She is pretty special."

"Remember when we married her?" Keegan said. "She cried because she wanted to be courted. That's what we need to do. We need to court her. Maybe she feels like she's been taken advantage of and she deserves more. Tomorrow morning the courting begins."

Alastair smiled in the darkness. "I like that idea. We should hold a dance. Do you think the ladies of Bridgewater would help us throw a party for our bride?"

"I just bet they would," Keegan said.

"Let's talk to the men and women first thing in the morning," Alastair said.

One of the new foals neighed. It was as if the horse was telling them to shut up and go to sleep.

"I like this plan," Alastair said. "I'm going to do everything I can to save this marriage. I want Catriona. But she needs to understand why I am so against scandal and cheating. I should have told her long before now."

21

The next morning, after she had bathed and fixed herself breakfast, she knew she needed to talk to the men. Last night, she'd been emotional. Learning that Charley, the man she loved and trusted had betrayed her, had been devastating. Suddenly she started to question if she was capable of knowing a good man from a bad one.

It seemed like she'd put all her faith and trust into the wrong one, and what if she had made a mistake in marrying Keegan and Alastair? Keegan seemed like a good man, but there was something about Alastair that left her bewildered. No matter what she did, she was not good enough for him.

A knock on the door had her running to answer it. She glanced out the window and saw three women from Bridgewater standing there.

She opened the door and they smiled at her. Georgia Hamilton stood before her. "Hi, Catriona, do you have a few minutes to talk?"

"Of course. Come on in," she said, inviting the women inside.

"I'm Mattie Craghead," a woman said.

"Your son went missing," Catriona said. "I was so happy when Keegan found him."

"Me too," the woman said.

"I'm Emma," a woman said. "I'm married to Whitmore and Ian."

"Please sit down," Catriona said, leading them into the living area.

"We're so glad you were found and safely brought home," Mattie said.

Catriona wasn't really ready to talk about what happened. She felt so confused and even humiliated that she had believed everything Charley told her.

"Thank you," she said.

Mattie reached out and took her hand. "Your husbands wanted us to come over and talk to you. They know you're upset with them."

"It was all so overwhelming. I should probably speak to them and let them know we need to talk."

Though she wasn't quite ready to give them an answer about their status just yet. She just needed a little more time to accept that while they were good men, she had to trust them and her faith in men had been shattered last night.

"No, they've gone to town to file a report with the new sheriff about Charley and Phillip," Emma said. "They wanted us to make certain you're all right."

How was she doing? How was one supposed to feel when their life had been threatened the night before? There was just so much confusion right now.

"I'm doing all right," she told the women. "It's just that a man I trusted very much betrayed me. He stole so much from me and killed my parents. That has made me question if I even know what a good man looks like. I'm just confused."

Emma nodded. "Any one of us would have been upset after what you went through. I think your men are afraid that you're going to give up on them."

The thought had crossed her mind, but yet her heart was very much involved. If she left them, she would be giving up on their marriage and she wanted it to work.

"Neither one of them has had to work hard to get me. They married me to protect me from Phillip and didn't have to court me or prove to me that they love me. Maybe I'm wrong, but I want my husbands to love me. To want to protect me and cherish what we have. Maybe I'm feeling like it's all a little one sided right now."

The women nodded.

Emma leaned forward. "Catriona, they are men. A little slow to show their feelings, but believe me, I think they have realized their mistake. They want us to hold a barn dance tonight, to welcome you to the community. They want to show off their wife to everyone."

Mattie nodded and laughed. "Alastair asked me to make certain that you did not leave before they returned. He's very worried about you."

"Where would I go?" Catriona said. "I have a ranch, but I'm going to need to hire someone new to take care of it. I just don't know what I should do."

Georgia patted her belly. "Oh, the baby just kicked me. You've just experienced a terrible ordeal where you said a man you believed in betrayed you. Don't make any rash decisions. Give your husbands some time."

With a sigh, Catriona smiled at the women. "Thank you. I still don't know what to do, but maybe right now is not the time to make a rash decision. And my husbands want to hold a barn dance?"

"Yes," Emma said. "They pleaded with us to convince you to stay for the dance."

"Keegan was quite distraught at the idea that you would leave before they returned from town."

Warmth filled her heart. She loved both men, but just wanted them to show her that they had feelings for her. Didn't she deserve loving men?

"I've got to get back to the children. Whitmore was kind enough to watch them while I came over here. And I'm making a big pot of stew for tonight's dance. The children are going to enjoy watching the adults dance."

Catriona stood and hugged each woman. "Thank you so much for coming over this morning. You've made me feel better, and I promise I won't make any rash decisions. I'll give my men a chance before I decide what is best for me."

"Be careful," Georgia said. "You could find yourself in my situation. Happily married with a second baby on the way."

The thought of a child made Catriona smile. "I would love that very much. But before I bring a child into this world, I want to make certain this is a good home to raise a family."

The women nodded.

"See you tonight," they called as they walked out the door.

Catriona smiled as she thought of what she could wear tonight. But all of her clothes were still at her ranch.

That afternoon there was another knock on the door and when Catriona opened the door, there was a box on the porch. Inside was a beautiful green dress with a note.

We want you to have a new dress tonight to wear. With

your permission, we'd like to pick you up and escort you to the dance. If that is acceptable to you, then tie this pink handkerchief on the door.

She took her time preparing for the evening and when she was ready, Catriona tied the pink handkerchief on the door.

Within a few minutes, they appeared on her doorstep. She opened the door to stare at her two handsome husbands.

"Good evening, gentlemen," she said with a smile. "Thank you for the lovely dress. That was very thoughtful."

"That dress looks gorgeous on you," Keegan said.

Alastair took her in his arms. "You're going to be the prettiest girl at the dance."

A smile spread across her face and she took each man by the arm.

"Let's go," she said and then she halted a frown crossing her face. "I have to know one thing before I can go any farther. Are we going to be safe tonight? Are Phillip and Charley in jail?"

The two men grinned.

"They won't be seeing daylight anytime soon. The new sheriff may want to speak to you next week, but they're behind bars," Keegan said.

"You don't ever have to worry about being safe again. We'll always protect you," Alastair said. "We will guard you with our lives."

"Then yes, please take me to the dance," she said. "Let's have fun tonight."

When they walked through the barn door, she saw the women had made an archway out of lace and ribbon.

The crowd grew quiet when they entered.

"People of Bridgewater, we'd like to introduce you to our wife, Catriona O'Reilly Black, bride of Keegan and Alastair," Keegan announced.

The people clapped and smiled, and one by one, came over and introduced themselves to Catriona. A feeling of welcome overcame her and she leaned on her husbands for their support.

Finally, the band began to warm up and Alastair turned to her.

"May I have the first dance," Alastair said.

"Yes," she said. It was hard with Alastair because all she could think about was how he had not helped Keegan save her. She wanted to ask him where he was and knew that before they could move forward, she needed answers.

The band began to play a tune and the two of them waltzed onto the floor. He held her close, enjoying the feel of his arms around her, though her body was tense. "Catriona, promise me that sometime tonight we can talk. There are things I need to tell you. But tonight, we want you to enjoy yourself and have fun. We want to show you off to the people of Bridgewater."

A feeling of hope began to build inside her. Maybe she would finally learn why he was so withdrawn from her. Why he couldn't seem to trust her.

Slowly, she relaxed in his arms and when the dance was over he took her over to Keegan.

"Oh, Catriona, you, my dear wife, are the belle of the ball tonight. We're so proud that you're our wife," Keegan said and she smiled at him. "Tonight is all about you."

A smile crossed her face. "Thank you, Keegan. You and Alastair have made me feel special and I appreciate that."

"Oh, honey, you are special. We recognized that about you the very first day we met. Those sweet foals are out in the pasture tonight, but they are what introduced us to you and for that we will forever be grateful."

Warmth began to spread through her. All night long, her husbands were right there, bringing her punch and food and making certain she had a place to sit when she tired.

It was like the two men woke up this morning and knew what they needed to do in order to save their marriage.

Tears welled in her eyes as she watched them and knew they were her life. There were no decisions to be made. She loved them and wanted to spend her life with them by her side.

People were beginning to leave. Children were being gathered and couples were starting for home.

Emma made her way to her and she shooed her husbands away.

"I hope that tonight you've had a great time," she said, taking her hands. "Your men are learning. Give them time."

Catriona pulled her into an embrace and hugged her. "Thank you. Thank you for making me feel welcome and for sharing with me. I think I've found my home."

Emma pulled back and smiled. "Good luck, tonight."

"Thank you," she said as her new friend walked away. The ladies of Bridgewater had accepted and welcomed her and she felt like she'd found her new life.

When her men returned, they gazed at her with uneasiness in their eyes.

"I'm ready for you to take me home," she said. "But I want you to know that tonight has been wonderful. Thank you for an excellent evening."

"Of course," Alastair said.

"We'll take you home," Keegan said.

22

*A*ll the way home, Alastair feared what she was going to say. Had he damaged their relationship to the point that she wanted nothing to do with them ever again? He hoped she would give him a chance to explain his actions.

When they stepped on the porch, Keegan opened the door and glanced at Alastair, as if to say *what do we do now?*

"Come in and let's talk," Catriona said. "We need to discuss our expectations in a marriage."

Funny, he remembered them having this conversation with her once before, but she had not given them her expectations.

They walked in the house and Keegan lit a lantern. He brought it into the living room and placed it on a table next to where she sat on the couch. Alastair sat next to her and Keegan paced the floor.

"I—" Alastair began, knowing he needed to tell her everything, but she interrupted him.

"I'm going first," she said. She took a deep breath. "Last night, I felt like all the men in my life had either betrayed me or tried to. Alastair, you didn't help Keegan rescue me and that was so disappointing. Phillip wanted to kill both of you, make me a widow, marry me and then kill me."

Shaking her head, she wiped a tear away. "Charley, the man who I believed was my second father, disappointed me the most. Not only did he kill my parents, but he destroyed my trust in men.

"When we got home, I just needed time away from everyone to make some decisions. I needed to clear my head and come to terms with what had happened. If you do not want to remain married to me, then you need to let me know now, because I can't deal with more heartache."

Alastair took her hand. "No, we want to remain married to you. I'm sorry, Catriona, for running last night. I was there by Keegan's side, but when I saw you undressed, it brought back painful memories, and like a coward, I ran."

For the next several minutes, he told her about his mother and what had happened with his family.

When he finished, he gazed into her emerald eyes

and knew his life was here with this woman by his side.

"If you'll forgive me, I promise I will trust you and love you until my dying day. You're the woman I want to love forever."

She sat there shaking her head. "I had no idea about your family, I'm sorry, Alastair. But hear me now." She took his other hand in hers. "You and Keegan will never have to worry about me cheating. You are my husbands and my heart belongs to both of you. Last night made me realize how much I love you. I want to be your wife and you will never have to worry about another man. Or scandal or anything else, because this is our home and here we will raise our children."

Keegan grinned. "Damn, I'm so happy. Catriona, I have loved you since the moment I saw you in that barn. For years, I've wanted a wife and a family. My mother and father deserted me on a street corner when I was five. For many years, I lived in an orphanage. Now I want to give a child a good home. Help me overcome my past with a great family life. You've made me so very happy. Does this mean we don't have to sleep in the barn tonight?"

"Both of you have never told me about your pasts. This helps me understand you and together we can ease our pain and create the family we want."

A smile crossed his wife's face and Alastair knew

she had forgiven him, and he had complete trust in her.

Slowly she stood. She kissed each man. And then she turned to the stairs. "I'll be waiting upstairs for you my husbands."

Warmth filled Alastair as he watched her walk up the steps.

"Damn, she loves us and I love her," he said.

Keegan grinned. "I knew you could do it. I knew you could learn to trust her."

"I do. Come on, let's fuck our wife. I can't wait," Alastair said with a grin.

23

She removed her clothes, got on the bed, and laid her forehead on her hands. In this position, with her ass up in the air, she waited for them. Anxious and yet now that she was in this position, she was also excited to think about their cocks entering her pussy.

In a moment, she heard their boots on the stairs and them talking low. They were up to something and she wasn't sure she was going to like it.

When they came in, she snuck a peek as they began to remove their clothing. The expressions on their faces were not of happiness or even joy.

"Before we begin, there is one small matter you are going to be punished for," Keegan said.

"What? Don't ruin what we're starting here," she said, fear suddenly filling her.

Alastair ran his hand over her buttocks. "Did you leave with Phillip?"

"You know I did. I thought I was saving Charley," she said.

"Didn't we tell you never to leave without telling us? That you are not to go anywhere alone?"

She bit her bottom lip. "All right, I disobeyed. What are you going to do?" Rolling over, she faced them as they pulled her up to stand.

"We're going to spank you," Alastair said.

"I would argue that I was trying to save someone I loved. Someone that betrayed me," she said, the painful memory overwhelming her. As much as she wanted to, she could not hold back the tears.

Charley's betrayal hurt. She had loved and trusted him since she was a child. All she wanted to do was protect him, stop Phillip, and save Charley.

A sob escaped her and both men were at her side.

"Oh, honey, don't cry," Keegan said, holding her tightly.

She sobbed on Keegan's shoulder and he rubbed her back. "You are my men. I love you and would die protecting you."

"Tonight, we won't punish you, but you have to obey us," Keegan said.

"I know," she said through her tears. "It's just I would try to save you. It's how I treat the people I love.

I thought I was saving Charley only to discover he wasn't who I thought he was."

Alastair stepped in behind her and hugged her. "Baby, we love you and don't want you to ever be in danger. You've got to trust us."

"And I do, but you also have to trust me."

"Agreed," Alastair said. "I promise you I'm going to trust you."

"Then don't spank me," she pleaded. "At least not hard."

The two men started to laugh. "Do you like it when we spank you for pleasure?"

"Yes," she said softly. "Just not when you do it hard."

She watched as Keegan glanced at Alastair. "Tonight should be about enjoying one another. Tonight should be fun. A celebration of our love, our life. Tonight I want us to create a baby."

The thought filled her with warmth and she thought of Georgia and how she was so excited for this baby to come. That could soon be her and she was eager to get started.

He wiped the tears from her eyes and pushed her onto the bed.

"Tonight, we take you at the same time," Alastair said, sinking down on the bed.

"Really? You think I'm ready?" she asked, fear filling her at the thought. Every day they had put a new butt plug in her, and every day she felt full.

"Oh yes," Keegan said. "And we can't wait to claim you together."

"Keegan will take your ass and I'm going to shove my cock in that sweet pussy of yours."

Alastair pulled her onto his lap and kissed her on the mouth, his lips moving over hers in a gentle way, sending fire spiraling through her.

She wanted her husbands and couldn't wait to experience both of them. But the thought was both chilling and thrilling.

He passed her to Keegan. "Darling, tonight we're going make you scream our names in pleasure."

The very though made her giggle. "I bet you can't."

"Oh, that is a wager you will lose," Keegan promised. "And we are going to spank you, but it will be to make you come. You are going to come a lot tonight."

"I can't wait," she whispered as she ran her hand down to his penis. It was hard and she stroked it with her hand. "Maybe I'll make you scream my name."

"Oh God, please do," Keegan said, gasping as she stroked his long member, knowing he would soon take her.

Alastair put his fingers between her legs and up her cunny.

"She's soaking wet," he said with a grin. "Oh, honey, I love that you get so excited."

Keegan kissed her, his mouth moving over hers, causing her to groan with need.

When they broke apart, he gazed at her. "On your knees."

She crawled up on the bed onto her knees.

He slapped her on the ass. "I'm claiming this sweet little butt tonight. I'm going to make it pink and you're going to beg me to take you."

With a glance over her shoulder, she taunted him. "My big strong man, you are not going to get what you want."

Keegan pushed her head down on the bed, raising her bottom into the air. Slowly, he pulled the last butt plug from her bottom. His fingers slid into her puckered hole so easily now, sending a tingle through her, causing her to gasp. Stroking her insides, she whimpered as he filled her with his fingers, stretching her, a rush of pure heat spiraled through her.

"Before I'm finished, you're going to be begging me."

"No," she taunted him and he slapped her on her ass. Passion filled her and she moaned.

Alastair moved in front of her and she stroked his cock near her face. "Catriona, suck me."

She opened her mouth and lovingly sucked the end of his cock, her tongue circling it. Keegan was behind her, spreading her legs.

His fingers brushed against her clit and then he

slapped her pussy, sending desire shooting through her. She almost came then.

With Alastair's cock in her mouth, she groaned as Keegan continued to stroke her. Alastair reached down and twisted her nipples and she gazed up at him, his cock in her mouth.

These were her men. Her protectors, her lovers, and her husbands, and she loved them with every fiber of her being. They were her reasons for living. With them, they would create a family and live here in Bridgewater.

Keegan twisted his fingers inside her ass and she all but screamed on Alastair's cock as heat flooded her and she moved her ass begging him for more.

"Oh, Catriona, I'm going to come," Alastair said. "Swallow it all."

At that moment, she felt him surge in her throat and she swallowed his seed as it pulsed inside her throat and she licked his cock as it slipped from her mouth.

Keegan plunged into her pussy and she clenched her muscles around his girth, wanting it, needing it, inside her. Ripples of pleasure spread through her and she knew that if she came, she would be in trouble.

Alastair moved beneath her and she knew they were preparing to take her both at the same time.

"Keegan," she cried. "Please, I'm going to come."

"No you're not, unless you want me to spank you

hard," he said, slapping her ass again. "I love how pink your cheeks are becoming. It makes me want to smack them again."

Gingerly, he rubbed his hand over her ass and then he smacked her twice.

"Oh," she cried.

Suddenly he pulled out of her and stopped. "Beg me, Catriona. Tell me how much you want my cock in your ass."

A groan rippled through her, she was right on the edge, just a few more moments and she would have been tumbling over the edge, spiraling out of control, but instead she leaned back trying to find his cock. Needing him.

"Please, Keegan fuck me in the ass. Hurry."

He leaned over her and kissed her back. "Darling, that's what I wanted to hear."

"I'll have you crying my name sometime tonight," she promised.

Alastair was stroking his cock and she could see that it was getting hard again and she knew he was going to put it in her pussy.

Glancing back over her shoulder, she cried. "Keegan, fill me."

"Of course," he said.

His penis was at her ass. They were truly going to take her, both at the same time. Fear and desire mixed through her and she felt him pushing. Without thinking, she tensed.

"Let me in, Catriona. Open for me," Keegan said, stroking her clit.

She sighed and relaxed against Alastair's chest as Keegan pushed his cock into her, filling her. He was so big, and even though they had prepared her, she felt like she was being ripped in two.

"Keegan," she cried suddenly fearing what they were doing to her. "Please, stop."

"A little more, darling, a little more and then you'll be all ours. We're going to claim you together."

She took a deep breath and tried to relax. Suddenly she felt Keegan glide the rest of the way in and his hips were against her buttocks.

"Oh," she cried, trying her best to relax. "I'm so full."

"Now my turn," Alastair said as he pushed into her pussy.

They were both inside her and she felt stuffed. These were her men, her lovers, and she loved that they were both claiming her. Now she was truly theirs.

"Darling, your ass is so tight. It feels so good," Keegan told her as he pulled out and then in again.

Alastair began a rhythm, with one going in and the other one pulling out. He reached up and sucked her nipple into his mouth, his teeth nipping her puckered bud.

The bed began to move with their rhythm and Catriona felt like she would explode as the passion consumed her. Flames burned her as she rocked with their bodies.

"Keegan, Alastair," she cried as the heat begin to spin through her, the walls of her pussy clenching. "Fuck me."

"Don't come yet," Keegan warned. "I want to hear you screaming my name."

"Mine too," Alastair said as he pinched her nipples before his mouth claimed hers.

Never did she imagine that being taken by them both would leave her feeling so out of control, like any moment, she would melt right here in their arms.

"Now you're ours," Alastair said, his voice rough. "You belong to us. Only us."

"Yes," she cried. "I'm yours. I'm going to come."

"Not yet," Keegan said. "We're all coming at the same time."

"Keegan..." she cried, trying to hold back but couldn't stop the orgasm.

"Go ahead, darling, you deserve it," Keegan said as he popped her on the buttocks, sending her over the edge.

With a scream, she felt her insides tighten and her muscles ripple around their cocks. "Oh, Keegan, Alastair."

"Yes," Keegan said. "Grip my cock with your muscles."

Alastair pushed deep, spasming inside her as his seed coated the walls of her pussy.

"Cat," he groaned.

Keegan slapped her on the ass once again and this time she felt him slam into her, his seed coating her, groaning as he leaned over her.

"You're ours," he said as he convulsed around her. "Our names are branded on your heart."

"Yes," she whimpered as she lay spent, slowly coming back down to earth.

The smell of sex filled the room as they all three collapsed. Catriona lay between her cowboys. These were her husbands and her life would revolve around them and that's what she wanted.

"Next time you're going to scream my name," she whispered.

"Yes," Keegan agreed.

"Rest and we'll do it again," Alastair said. "I can't wait to stick my cock in your ass."

Lying between them, all she could think about was that today, they had confessed their love for one another. Today, they had pledged themselves to one another.

"You're my cowboys," she said. "And I love you."

Nothing would ever come between them.

24

Keegan held her hand and Alastair held the other. "Come on honey, push."

The look she gave Keegan should have frightened him. In the months since they had moved everything from her ranch to their house, he had learned his wife had a fiery temper when she didn't like something.

"What do you think I'm doing?"

Alastair moved behind her. "Lean against me and I'll hold you up as you push."

"That's a girl," the midwife said.

"Aargh," she screamed as she gave one last big push.

"We're almost there," the midwife said. "I see a crown."

"Aargh," she screamed again and then suddenly she went limp.

"Cat," Keegan screamed.

The midwife laughed. "A boy."

"Is my wife all right," Keegan demanded.

Cat opened her eyes and stared at Keegan. "Love, I'm tired."

"We have a son," Alastair told her and she gazed at her husbands and grinned.

The midwife clipped the umbilical cord and began to clean the mucus from the baby's face. The little boy howled his dislike, his body going stiff.

"The next one should be a girl," she said weakly.

"Oh, he has his mother's Irish temper," Keegan said.

"Our world will never be the same," Alastair said as he gazed at their son.

When he was clean, the midwife wrapped the child in a blanket and handed him to his mother.

"Oh, look at him. He's beautiful."

"Nay, he's not beautiful, he's a handsome son," Alastair said, wiping the tears from his eyes. "And he's going to have the best damn life."

Catriona reached up and ran her hand down her husband's cheek. "Yes, he will. His mother will love and protect him and his fathers will show him how to be a good man."

Alastair leaned into her hand and kissed her palm. "I love you more than the air I breathe."

"Me too," Keegan said. "We should name him Kac.

Keegan, Alastair, and Catriona. He's a combination of us three."

"No, I think he should be called, Reilly. Because of O'Reilly's Folly, we came together," Catriona said gazing at her husbands.

"I kind of like that," Keegan said.

"Me too," Alastair said. "Reilly Black. May he have a blessed life with parents who adore him."

"Love you my husbands," Catriona said as she gazed down at their son. "Thank you for giving me this beautiful life."

Want more Bridgewater Brides?
See the full list of books in the world:
http://bridgewaterbrides.com/books/

THANK YOU!

Dear Reader,
Thank you for coming on this journey with me. As a writer every story is an experience and I'm so thankful that Vanessa allowed me to write in her world. If you're looking for more stories, please check out my other romances.

If you'd like to learn about my new releases before anyone else, sign up for my new book alerts.

Again, thanks for reading my books.
Lacey Davis

Happily Ever After is Different for Everyone

Email — AuthorLaceyDavis@outlook.com

ABOUT THE AUTHOR

Lacey Davis is a pseudonym for a USA Today bestselling author who wanted to try her hand at writing sexy romance. With these novels, I hope to write sizzling romances that will leave you grabbing a fan to cool yourself off.

If you like hunky bad boy heroes who like to be in charge and strong pretty women who are willing to risk it all, then look no further. These sexy reads will get you in the mood. Come experience strong women who will tame these bad boys and leave them wanting more.

Goodreads — https://www.goodreads.com/author/show/7985938.Lacey_Davis

WANT MORE LACEY DAVIS?

How about another Lacey Davis romance?

Two Texas Rangers and one wild bride?

Unmarried and alone is dangerous in the wilds of Texas. Lillian Bradley's family died leaving her to run the ranch that her lowlife neighbor covets. And someone is stealing her cattle. She needs a protector, a husband, and she needs him now.

Texas Rangers Will and Seth are looking for a gunslinger. They ride into Blessing just as a bank robbery is occurring. Only the thief isn't the feisty blonde woman they accuse. With one look, they know she will be theirs, that they will cherish, protect, and love her.

Is Lillian the key to finding their suspect and is she the woman who will satisfy their longings? Or will a family tie from the past destroy the life they're creating?

Get Loving My Cowboys now!

Read the first chapter!

Lillian Bradley sat astride a large red mare, gazing out at Texas's rolling hills, counting the cattle for a third time. Someone was stealing her cows.

With a sigh, her eyes roamed across the land she loved. All this acreage, cattle, goats, horses, and even a bunch of chickens, but they were all she had. Lilly was alone.

Yellow fever had raced through her family, killing everyone but herself. Alone, she didn't understand how she had survived, but here she was with a large ranch and no one to help her with the many chores and responsibilities.

Some days, it was more than a body could bear, but she refused to give it up.

Dust rose in the distance and she watched as a rider rode toward her. As the stranger drew closer, a groan rose in her throat. Jim White of the Big W Ranch, her neighbor, was coming for a visit.

The man owned the largest spread in this section

of Texas and was known for his shady deals, swindling, and even his prostitutes.

Her hand lingered on the rifle she had become accustomed to being at her side.

He pulled his horse up beside her. "Good morning, Miss Bradley. How are you today?"

She turned and gave him an irritated frown. The wind blew her blonde hair into her face and she brushed it back. "Someone is stealing my cattle."

"I'm sorry to hear that," he said. "You know, a pretty young woman like yourself shouldn't be worrying over lost cattle."

"Maybe not, but yellow fever didn't give me much choice."

Her mare shimmied nervously, her paws dancing, eager to get away.

"Let me buy the ranch from you. Or even better, have you considered my son Matt? You are of marrying age. We could combine our land together into one big family ranch."

Like hell. She would shoot herself before she'd marry his weasel son.

"Thank you, but I'm not selling my family's land. Their deaths will not be in vain. As for marrying your son, no thank you."

It was all she could do to keep from screaming *oh hell no*. Not Matt White, a mean, cussing, tobacco spitting boy who knew his father would always get him out of trouble.

Mr. White's face turned red and his lips pressed into a thin line, but she didn't care. "A young woman should not be running a ranch."

"And yellow fever should not have killed my family." She sighed and turned to him. "For the last six months, I've taken care of this ranch and I plan on continuing. Need to find a new helper since Mr. Bennett disappeared."

The man was like family and she was so disappointed he left her when she needed him the most. For nearly fifteen years, the man worked on the ranch and then one day, he just vanished.

"Miss Bradley," Jim said, his voice coaxing and gentle. "I could take the worry off your hands. You would be free to be the young woman you long to be."

It was true that she pined to have a carefree life again. One where all she had to worry about was helping her mother with dinner or the laundry. Where her grandmother baked a cake every week. Her grandfather and she went fishing when the weather permitted. But those days were gone. Stolen from her by a hideous disease.

"I'm so glad you came by, Mr. White. If you know anything about who might be taking my cattle, tell them I'm a fine shot with a rifle and I will not hesitate to kill them. Also, if you see my helper, Mr. Bennett, tell him I would like to talk with him about increasing his salary."

Often times, she worried something had happened to Mr. Bennett. Because she didn't think he would have left without saying goodbye. At least, she hoped not.

"Will do, Miss Bradley. You think about my offer. I'm willing to give you top dollar for your ranch."

Top dollar, her ass. The man was a known cheat and would not give her anything for the Rockin' B Ranch. Over the years, her father had complained how when times got bad, Ole Jim was there to steal the property for little or nothing from the ranchers in dire straits.

"Good day, Mr. White."

It was a clear signal for him to leave. She had an appointment with the banker later today and she needed to be riding into town but would wait until he was out of sight. Though she doubted he would do something, she could see him setting fire to the house to force her to sell.

The man was a vulture of the worst kind. Preying on the weak and, right now, she was in his sights.

What she needed was a husband. Someone to help her with the ranch. To keep rustlers from cutting the fence and stealing her herd. Someone to fill the house with love and laughter. Someone to help her create her own family.

The big house was empty and creaked and moaned

at night. Fear had her sleeping on the horsehair couch her mother had been so proud of.

While she had managed on her own for six months, it was time for her to fill her bed. Someone to teach her the ways between a man and a woman. Someone to scratch this itch she knew only a man could fulfill. And she wanted someone to love her and the Rockin' B.

Glancing down at the dress she wore, she'd donned her prettiest. This morning she bathed, fixed her hair with the hot iron, and made certain she looked her best.

She knew what she had to do. After she went to the bank, she planned on talking to the preacher about any eligible young men who might be interested in her as a wife.

It was time to go husband hunting. It was time to find herself a man.

Get Loving My Cowboys now!